OMEGA MINE

Search for a Soulmate

by
LETA BLAKE

An Original Publication from Leta Blake Books
Originally written and published in 2018 by Lucky Honey Books under the pen name Halsey Harlow
Cover by Dar Albert
Formatted by BB eBooks

First Edition, 2018
Second Digital Edition, 2020
ISBN: 979-8-88841-065-3

Can an Alpha find his dream Omega on reality TV?

Alpha Hank Morrow is a bear shifter who has never found the right Omega. Without the steadying influence of a bond with his Omega, Hank's powerful Alpha senses are beginning to overwhelm and endanger not only him, but his fellow police officers and the entire city of White Edge. The chief of police and the governor sign Hank up for a reality TV show to help unmatched Alphas find their dream Omega.

Omega Mine: Search for a Soulmate certainly isn't Hank's idea of a great plan, but he's not given a choice. Now he's off to a tropical island to meet over one hundred potential Omegas in a televised version of hell.

Or is it?

Evan Vaughn is an unmatched Omega. He and Hank have actually met once before at an Alpha-Omega mixer, but he didn't make much of an impression at the time. Will that change on the set of *Omega Mine*? And can anything real come out of a reality TV dating show? Hank and Evan are about to find out…

***The Bachelor* meets Alpha-Omega romance!**

This book is nearly 40,000 words of an oblivious bear shifter finally meeting his match with a happy ending you'll love!

For B, with all my heart

CHAPTER ONE

SITTING ON THE ground at the head of a circle carved into the surrounding jungle, a fire roaring in front of him, Hank was overheated despite being shirtless. They were bringing in the Omega applicants now. One by one, they filed in front of him, some wearing somber, alert expressions, others smiling at him hopefully, and one dancing along to the drums, shaking his body to the sound, smiling up at the sky, not even looking toward Hank at all.

Hank wiped a hand over his face, ostensibly to clear off the sweat that poured from him, but mainly to clear his sight of it all for a moment. The night was surreal, and he felt himself slipping a little, losing control of his reactions and senses; the fire flickered a little too rhythmically and the drums pulsed around him. He could easily slip into an Alpha trance and shift if he wasn't careful.

That was why he was here. He needed one of these idiots to keep Alpha trances and unpredictable shifts from happening on the job. He glanced around the fire at the now seated applicants, each one of them staring at him with wide, eager eyes. A few attempted a smile, and the one who'd been dancing joyfully on his own grinned and bobbed his head to the beat.

Hank sighed. It wasn't like he hadn't tried to find an Omega on his own. He'd gone to those damn mixers that his non-shifter boss David, the chief of White Edge police, had insisted on arranging for him through the Omega Program at the local university.

Was it Hank's fault that the people who attended those weren't for him? As he told David after the last mixer, "Two had a cat, another a dog…" Hank had a strict bias against an Omega with animals. His allergies and sensitivities, not to mention potential of shifting into a predator, would necessitate the disposal of the animal and that seemed unnecessarily cruel. "Another smelled of Milk Bones, even though he did *not* have a dog…" Hank had looked at David pointedly. "Do I even need to say it?"

"Oh, yes, Hank, clearly a deviant," David had scoffed.

Hank had grunted and turned his back. "I just didn't feel it," he'd finally admitted. "I gotta feel it, David."

"Of course, you gotta feel it, Hank," David had said, slapping him on the shoulder. "I wouldn't marry a woman unless I felt it, and Alphas shouldn't take an Omega unless they feel it. I hear ya. The problem is, Hank, the council isn't 'feeling it' either. They've taken it directly to the governor and word has come down that you need an Omega. You're too big of a risk out on assignment any more without one."

"I know," Hank said, wanting to dispute it, but the last time had been too close. He'd tranced and ten men had nearly died. Men with wives and children, men with moms and dads, or girlfriends or even boyfriends, dammit. Men with *families*. He shook his head and sat down at David's office table.

"Look, Hank," David said, sitting across from him. "I know you aren't going to like it, but, hear me out, okay? The governor has insisted, as a show of good faith, as a serious gesture to prove that you are really looking for an Omega and not just pretending to look—"

"Pretending to look? For God's sake, David, why would I do that?" Hank demanded.

"You wouldn't. But the governor doesn't know that. And there's more to it, I think. Ratings. Money."

"Ratings?"

"Yes, ratings, Hank. They've got three other Alphas looking for Omegas. One Heather Kallet from Seattle, a tiger shifter, a Fong Wu from Paris, panther shifter, yes, I know rather unusual, but true all the same, and the last is…ahh"—David flipped through the packet of paper he held in his hands—"Cameron Cooper, a female mountain lion shifter, from Atlanta. All three have had an exceedingly difficult time 'feeling it', as you've put it, and all are in a position now where their future careers depend entirely on finding someone they can 'feel it' with." David cleared his throat and looked at Hank pointedly. "Sound familiar?"

Hank narrowed his eyes and said nothing.

David went on. "What was it my ex-wife said to me once? Oh, yes. She said, 'David, we live in an entertainment age.' At the time she was talking about the blasted reporters trying to turn my murder case into a three-ring circus, but now I say it to you: Hank, we live in an entertainment age. Welcome to it."

He slapped down a packet in front of Hank.

"What's this?" Hank asked.

"It's your application. It's already been submitted by the governor and you'll be picked up on Thursday morning and flown to some sweet little island off the western coast of Mexico to participate in the first ever reality program featuring Alphas and Omegas."

"That's ridiculous."

"That's entertainment, Hank. Take it or—"

"I'll leave it, thanks," Hank said, shoving the packet back at David.

"I was going to say, 'Or kiss your career goodbye'."

David stood up, cocked his index finger at Hank like a gun,

and then left the room, leaving Hank's glare focused on the glass of the still shuddering office door.

Hank looked down at the glossy papers on the table. They were all imprinted with the same words: OMEGA MINE: SEARCH FOR A SOULMATE.

"Thank you for participating in the new reality program sponsored by CBS and the U.S. Government," Hank had read aloud before flinging the papers at the door. "Over my dead body."

And yet now here he sat, red paint smeared on his chest in a way that was nothing like his old friend and teacher Alpha Krushreet's tribal decoration. Though how he could expect the bastards in charge of these shenanigans to have any idea about actual, real traditional shifter tribes, he didn't know. The fire roared in front of him and the faces of thirty-five potential candidates gazed adoringly at him. He groaned under his breath at the crass naked hope that radiated from each of them.

Warren, the emcee, or Man With the Microphone, as he'd introduced himself to Hank earlier, sat down beside him wearing a red T-shirt and khaki shorts. "How are you feeling, Hank?" Warren asked, smiling roguishly and shoving the microphone in Hank's face. "Pretty excited?"

Hank said, "I could think of other words."

"Yeah? I bet you could. It must be amazing to sit here looking at each of these attractive, smart, interesting young people and know that every one of them is here for *you*, Hank. How does that feel?"

Damn creepy, Hank thought. "There are three other Alphas. I'm not the only one," he said. "So they're not here just for me."

"Right! Tonight, at three different sites on the island, far enough away to avoid territory issues, we have three other Alphas sitting at identical fires with another thirty-five faces staring at them as well. How do you imagine they're feeling?"

"Hot," Hank said, wiping his face. "And tired."

Warren laughed. "Oh, Hank, ever the straight man in the comedy duo."

Hank gave a tight-lipped smile at that and turned his focus back to the faces around the fire. He didn't see anyone of initial interest to him.

Warren talked on. "That's right, folks. Four Alphas with thirty-five applicants each. That's one hundred and forty applicants for only four Omega positions."

Warren threw his arm around Hank's shoulder and it was all Hank could do not to throw it off.

"For those in our viewing audience at home who might not be aware, an Alpha is a male or female shifter possessing the ability to change between their human form and an animal form—usually a wolf or a great cat, though some bear shifters, like Hank here, do exist. They're also blessed with extraordinary sensory abilities, far beyond the normal human's imagination. Those abilities allow them, no, compel them by forces written into their DNA to serve and protect their pack mates, which are, luckily for us, made up of regular old homosapiens like you and me. In other words, alphas are *super-human*."

Warren paused dramatically and Hank moved out from under his arm, glancing around, looking for a way out.

Warren continued his explanation, "But nature has a way of balancing things out. For, you see, every Alpha needs an Omega or he becomes a slave to his senses. He or she becomes unable to control them, and, as a result, can shift without warning or control. Thus, they can become a danger to themselves and the men or women who follow them into battle."

Hank looked at the large screen opposite showing the footage live as it aired. Warren's voiceover was being intercut with footage of Hank by the fire, the applicants, and a 're-enactment' of a police standoff going awry because the actor posing as the Alpha suddenly covered his eyes and began crying out, falling to the floor, and writhing there, computer-generated fur bursting out of his cheeks and hands.

Hank sneered, but his stomach twisted. As much as he wanted to dismiss what he'd seen as nothing more than bad acting, he remembered all too well the blood welling from Johnson's abdomen after Hank's vision had suddenly telescoped and then gone out entirely during the last bust he'd led. At least he hadn't shifted.

Warren talked on, "But finding an Omega isn't an easy task. Oh, no, ladies and gentlemen, being an Omega requires so much more than just the skills required to perform in the field, such as using a firearm or basic self-defense; there must be a *connection* between Alpha and Omega, a connection those of us who are mere mortals—"

Hank rolled his eyes. He was mortal for God's sake.

"Those of us who are mere mortals can barely imagine. A *soul* connection."

Hank looked at Warren in disgust. He didn't like thinking about souls, much less soul connections. He wasn't even sure he believed in such a thing. He just knew that when he met the person he wanted as his Omega, then he had to trust the person, completely, and he had to want them to know him in every way. And, some primitive part of him that he wanted to dismiss but simply couldn't, knew that he'd want to fuck the person. And not just a regular old screw, either. But a deep, serious, intense, mind-blowing fuck. And he knew that he'd want to fuck his Omega like that as often as possible for the rest of his life.

"Yes, that's what this is, folks. That's what these Alphas are here for. They're looking for the *one* Omega for them. They might be different from us in many ways: better, stronger, faster. They might grow a fuzzy fur coat and run on four legs when they shift. But in one very intimate and important way they are just the same: they need love to light their way."

Hank covered his mouth and coughed at Warren's syrupy nonsense.

Love? It wasn't love. It was something else. He couldn't describe it. He wasn't great with words, but love was what he'd felt for his ex-wife before it'd gone south. No, whatever he'd have with his Omega was something deeper than that, and as he looked out at the faces flickering in the firelight, he knew he wasn't going to find it in any one of them. The person he chose for his Omega? They'd never look at him like *that*.

"And now we'll go to Margaret in Alpha Kallet's camp. Margaret? How's it going over there?"

The moment they were no longer on the air, Warren stood up and walked away. Hank heaved a sigh of relief, grateful to be escorted from the fire and into the air-conditioned resort. He would've been happy to go to bed, wake up the next morning to a nice breakfast of fruit and bagels, and then hop the next flight back to White Edge.

Instead, he was told to prepare himself for the meet and greet portion of the evening.

CHAPTER TWO

A N HOUR AND a half later, Hank had his shirt on. That was an improvement, at least.

He looked around the resort's ballroom, which CBS and the government had spent way too much money on in order to make it look like a jungle. Which made no sense because he was a bear shifter, and his animal preferred a mountainous, evergreen forest. Not this nonsense. He felt hemmed in and caged.

Everywhere he turned he saw only face after open, eager, face floating on an endless sea of noise. There were shoes scuffling, tapping, and moving. There were fingers cracking and popping in nervous tics, noses being blown, hiccups being fought off, and loud bursts of voices, all accompanying the thick and pervasive scent of excitement and worry.

It was all too much, and it seemed like the evening would never be over. Hank was desperate to slip away from the men and women who followed him relentlessly, attempting to anticipate his needs before he could even think of them. He held up his hand to prevent a group of them from following him any farther once he reached the door he'd been searching for and said, "I think I can make it to use the facilities on my own, thanks. A little privacy, please."

The bathroom was like heaven, quiet and dimly lit. The noise from the crowd drifted under the door in waves of sound that rushed around his feet. He could tolerate that, even relax into the pull of it a little. He sat his drink on the flat edge of one of the big, bowl-shaped enamel sinks and sank down into one of the soft chairs beside them.

He sighed deeply and put his head back. God, this was hell. Pure and simple. Women and men tugging at him, asking him to smell them, smiling at him with intent, *talking* to him, asking questions, *wanting answers*, he didn't know how things could get much worse.

The flush of the toilet surprised him, but only a little. He realized that he'd been subconsciously aware there was a person who'd just urinated in the stall, but it hadn't registered enough to bother him. He lifted his head and watched with amusement as the kid with long, curly brown hair—the one who'd danced around the fire—jumped in surprise to see Hank sitting there.

"Jeez, man!" the kid yelped, a hand going instinctively to his chest and his eyes flying wide. "Make a little noise or something!"

Hank fought a smile and said, "My apologies. Didn't mean to scare you."

"Right," the guy said, going to the sink to wash his hands. "Of course not. Apology accepted."

As he washed thoroughly, Hank studied him.

He wasn't a kid, really, Hank supposed. Probably thirty years old, more or less. Still, something about him struck Hank as kid-like, and he didn't change Hank's opinion when he pulled several paper towels out of the dispenser to wipe his hands, saying, "Paper, funny thing about paper—used to be everyone was worried about using too much paper, so they put those hand blowers in everywhere. You know those hand blowers, man?" He curved one hand and stuck the other under it, making a loud lawn-mower type noise. "Loud as anything. I'm sure you noticed. They promoted them like the end-all and be-all of progressive public bathroom design. They said they were cleaner and cost less and saved trees. Win-win for the whole world!"

The kid threw his hands up and tipped his head back in a gesture of exalted victory. Then he tipped his head back down, still smiling, and said, "Anyway, now they say that they're disease vectors that just blow the germs around, and if the filters aren't changed enough, and you know how it is, man, they never are, then they are basically nothing more than ebola outbreaks waiting to happen! That's the way it always is—cultures adapt and change and then return to old ways." He held up the paper towels in his hands as evidence.

Hank would have thought the kid was a hypochondriac except that he looked pretty damn cheerful, as though what he really found fascinating was the *story* he was telling, rather than any true concern about the spread of disease through hand blowers in bathrooms.

"Wow," Hank said, without much feeling behind it. "I take it that before applying to be an Omega on a reality TV show you were in the paper towel business, Captain?"

The kid laughed with his whole body, throwing his head back to reveal a strong throat with an Adam's apple that bobbed vulnerably. When he stopped chuckling, he said with a grin, "No, of course not." Then he stepped forward, stuck out his hand, and said, "Evan Vaughn. Cultural Anthropologist and fledgling professor."

Hank shook his hand and said, "Detective Hank Morrow, White Edge PD. Not a fledgling anything."

Vaughn chuckled again. "I know, man, remember? You're kinda the reason I'm here."

Hank felt as though he'd been dropped back into his body from a great height. It was an odd sensation, one that left him feeling leaden and flat. He realized that, yes, for the last several seconds while listening to Vaughn talk, he'd forgotten about the applicants shifting restlessly outside of the door, the voices murmuring competitively over who would get to speak with him next, each vying for his time and attention.

"Right, of course," Hank said, and rubbed the bridge of his nose.

At the end of the night, he was supposed to choose fifteen that he wanted to keep around for a second night and reject fifteen that would then be sent on to the other Alphas. He didn't know how he was going to even begin to do that. He couldn't remember a single name. Except this kid's.

Vaughn. Evan Vaughn.

"So, what's the score?" Evan asked. "Have you met anyone interesting?"

Hank looked at him hard and said nothing.

"Oh, come on. I'm not trying to get any info from you that you don't want to give. Listen, I doubt you're going to be interested in me anyway." Vaughn smiled, chuckling a little. "My research says that you're more into leggy and blonde than short and hairy, so I'm pretty sure I won't be on your list tonight, and we both know it."

Evan dropped into the matching chair on the opposite side of the sinks and gazed cheerfully across the two and a half feet between them. "So, is there anyone out there that you think might fit your bill?"

Hank cleared his throat and said, "Not that I recall. No."

Evan seemed empathetic. He leaned forward with his elbows on his knees, hands dangling between. His blue eyes were wide and his brows drawn low sadly. "That bad, huh?"

Hank shrugged and aimed to look unconcerned.

"Maybe in the next batch, then? Who knows?" Evan reached out and touched Hank's knee, a warm gesture, and he smiled. "You gotta keep your hopes up, man. I mean, surely out of one hundred and forty Omegas there'll be someone you click with, right? Positive attitude. It's more powerful than you think."

"Right-o, Captain. Good pep talk," Hank said sarcastically and felt a small, strange peace when Evan didn't seem to react to his tone at all. Not a flinch, not even a moment taken to reinforce his still-present smile.

Evan shrugged and said, "Okay, so don't panic. I'll tell you what, if you get up there and blank out, just look my way and I'll feed you names, okay? People I've met tonight and liked. What do you say?"

Hank raised a brow. "I say I can handle it on my own. Thanks."

"Oh, yeah, totally," Evan said, smiling and standing up. "Of course you can. Never said you couldn't." He stood up then and walked toward the door, pausing before pushing it open, "But remember—if you blank out, I'm your man."

The cacophony of voices raised in hopeful expectation dropped to angry tones when they realized that the person exiting the bathroom was *not* the Alpha but another Omega applicant who had just scored alone time with the object of their fixations.

Hank stayed in the restroom for another minute only standing up to leave when other applicants decided to ignore his request for privacy and sought one-on-one audiences with him as well, opening a floodgate of sudden bathroom urges in nearly everyone. Hank pressed through the crowd and out to the ballroom again, glad that the night was almost over.

As it turned out, when the time came and he stood sweating on the stage they'd erected amongst the fake vines and palm trees, he couldn't remember any names at all. A clinging and grinning Warren held the microphone in front of his face and urged him to choose someone from the crowd.

"Who floats your boat?" Warren asked on a chuckle.

Sweat slipped down Hank's back. He threw his gaze desperately around the room. Hadn't he thought the girl in blue was kind of smart? Or was it the one in purple? What about that guy wearing the cowboy hat? Had he thought he was funny? At least funny enough for one more day in his presence, or was that the guy he'd wanted to slug for making a stupid joke about the economy? He knew with a deep certainty that he'd rather be having a root canal, or ten of them, than standing there trying to choose between people he didn't know or even care to know.

His eyes landed on Evan, who was motioning desperately at the woman in front of him, mouthing something like the name Debbie or Dabby, probably the first and not the latter, and in a rush of relief at knowing someone's name, Hank said, "Evan Vaughn."

A collective undercurrent of a released breath ran through the room, though nothing loud enough that anyone other than Hank might hear.

Evan looked stunned, but he quickly said, "Okay, um, yeah. Okay, man. Hold on." He took a big gulp of his drink and sat it down before taking the stairs up to the stage two at a time.

Hank's hands were sweating and his heart was beating so hard that he was afraid he might start to trance on it. He didn't know how he felt about having chosen Evan first. He wondered if the guys back at the station would think he'd gone a little queer, if they would think that Evan was his *favorite*, when it'd only been desperation that had made him say the name.

"And your next choice, Alpha Morrow?" Warren asked, and Hank darted his eyes around, looking for anyone who didn't repulse him. The blonde that Evan had pointed at…maybe.

"Debbie," he said, and she smiled broadly, nodded graciously at him, and mouthed "Thank you" before joining him and Evan on the stage.

Evan stood to the right of him, and Hank turned to look at

him, wishing that Evan could feed him some more names, but it would be too obvious now.

Evan lifted his eyebrows and smiled, scooting a little closer to Hank. He whispered too softly for anyone else to hear, "Lots of B names here tonight, by the way."

B names? Hank coughed. B names. He tried to think of a B name. "Evan," he said.

Warren chuckled, "Yes, we understand that you liked Mr. Vaughn, but you've already chosen him for tonight's short list."

Nervous rustling around the room, and Hank felt panic rising. He should have paid more attention. He closed his eyes, took a deep breath. He could smell something warm and soothing, surprising because everyone was supposed to have bathed thoroughly in unscented products before they arrived.

He exhaled and remembered standing with a young brunette woman who had a kind smile. Her name had been....

"Markie," he said, and opened his eyes, hoping he'd gotten it right. He had, and her smile was still kind as she made her way up to the stage, her green shirt and brown pants hugging some nice curves as well.

He closed his eyes again, took another breath, and again found the scent that centered him. A flash of jeans and brown eyes, something about the girl had made him feel less anxious than some of the others.

"Barbara," he said. A B name. He glanced at Evan and gave him a very small smile.

Evan nodded and mouthed, "That's it."

Hank chuckled a little, feeling a wave of relief rush over him. He could do this. He only had twelve more names to go.

Oh God.

Closing his eyes again, the names came to him with small rushes of memory—a soft hand was Melinda, a soothing voice belonged to Bernice, and Joe had the cowboy hat and he was funny after all, or at least not annoying, and Bobby was a woman with a Southern accent and blonde hair, and Bitty was a little chubby and somehow smelled like vanilla wafers, and Hank liked vanilla wafers.

It went on until he'd chosen fifteen applicants to move to the next level. It seemed so arbitrary, ridiculous even, and yet he had to choose. It was part of the program. He kept waiting for something, waiting to feel "it," but a moment of lust never hit him. He decided that maybe it would happen with the next group of Omegas.

Tomorrow he'd spend fending off this group of fifteen. After that, he'd choose only three to stay for one-on-one dates, and then those three would return to him after they had visited all of the other Alphas, and, concurrently, the groups now with the other Alphas had visited him.

At that point, it had to be whittled down even more, several more one-on-one dates would take place, and then Hank would have to meet some of the applicants' families. It made Hank tense to even think about that.

But at least he'd made it through the night. Thanks to Evan Vaughn.

CHAPTER THREE

DAVID TUNED INTO the first episode along with everyone else in the White Edge Police Department. They'd all agreed that Tuesday night, come hell or high water, everyone would try to make time to watch the show together in the break room of the station, and as police chief he wasn't about to miss it.

Everyone crowded in, from his assistant Ellie, to her pal from staffing Chantal, to officers from Hank's team, Ben and Lee. There wasn't a single person in the station from the secretarial pool to fellow officers who weren't happy to have their thirst for information about their secretive Alpha, Hank Morrow, finally quenched.

"He's always been so mysterious," Chantal said to Ellie, voicing what everyone was thinking. "When he was first assigned to us as Alpha, I knew he was going to be great at protecting White Edge, but I assumed he'd be more gregarious. Like Alpha Elden was before him. Remember?"

Elden had been their prior Alpha. A fellow bear shifter, he had been much chummier with his co-workers. Retired now, he lived with his Omega in the woods far outside White Edge, where they were raising a family of foster-cub shifters and adopted human children. Elden kept his nose out of White Edge PD work now, though, knowing too well the violence that could come from a perceived challenge to Hank's authority.

"Show your Alpha respect," David said with irritation. "He is who he is, and we're lucky to have him."

Chantal ducked her head in submission and dropped the subject.

But truth be told, David was as curious as she was about Hank Morrow. His heart beat a little faster as the opening credits of *Omega Mine* began to roll.

The show itself started out rather dull. The four Alphas were introduced to the audience, including some shots of them at home with voice-overs about why they were looking for an Omega.

Cameron, Heather, and Fong all had a lot to say on the matter. Especially Fong who waxed lyrical on the subject while boating down the Seine, gazing wistfully into the water. His physique and his sensitive nature had the women in the room swooning immediately, and all of them whispered rueful questions like, "Why can't *our* Alpha be like *that*?"

Hank was featured in the middle of the group, as though the producers were hoping to downplay his taciturn nature by cramming him between the other three beautiful, talented, and vivacious Alphas.

His at-home-in-White Edge shots mainly captured him leaning over the railing of a bridge, watching the people pass below, looking serious and possessive of everything around him. "This is my home," he said. "These are the people I protect. I guess I need an Omega so I can keep on doing that."

David rolled his eyes. Hank sounded so lifeless and boring, so uncommitted. What television viewer, much less prospective Omega, was going to be lured in by that? Really, he was a hopeless case. David could only hope that Hank would somehow find someone just as boring as he was to take him on. So long as he and his Omega were committed to protecting White Edge, David couldn't care less who it was that Hank ended up with. Though, he supposed, as a friend, he hoped Hank would be happy with his choice.

A few Omegas were interviewed briefly, though there was a longer segment dedicated to an Evan Vaughn who'd apparently been studying Alphas for a while and was working on his doctorate in Cultural Anthropology with a thesis dedicated to the subject.

"All tribes of people since the beginning of time had an Alpha. A shifter who protected them and patrolled the borders of their lands…" Evan began, and he elaborated as the cameras followed him around a green, wet-looking campus that looked suspiciously like White Edge's own Spruce University.

"It's fascinating, really, the way that Alphas are drawn to the boundaries, and I mean that both physically and psychologically. They're the type of people you'll find dealing with the fringes of society, like drug dealers or prostitutes, because that's where the bad things happen. That's where the outside predators can break through and cause problems for their people. That's why so many Alphas excel in careers in law enforcement or the military. The black-and-white rules help them maintain their own boundaries, even when dealing with the criminal element."

Shortly thereafter it was revealed that, yes, Evan Vaughn was a graduate student and junior professor at Spruce.

"Why, that's right here in White Edge," Chantal exclaimed from across the room.

"Wonder if they ever met before the show?" Ben asked, voicing David's own curiosity. "You know, Hank and this Evan guy."

David thought that if Hank had met Evan at one of the mixers arranged through the university, then he was sure to be immediately out of the running. Which was too bad, because the kid seemed to have a handle on Alphas and what made them tick, something that David hadn't expected from someone so young and energetic.

The first episode concluded with each Alpha picking their fifteen applicants to spend time with the following day. Heather Kallet, beautiful and charming, seemed to have no problem choosing her fifteen, and while Fong was eloquent and poetic about how difficult it was to choose between so many amazing people, he didn't seem that perplexed by the question of who to give the ax to in the end. Cameron was methodical and systematic, having made notes with a rating system, marking a score by each name. Hank, however, hadn't seemed to put forth much of an effort the entire evening, and was now obviously panicking.

When Hank blurted out Evan's name, it became clear that some of the guys in the room weren't watching the show because they hoped Hank found the right Omega for him, but rather because they hoped to live vicariously.

"Aw, man, he didn't choose that brunette with the great ta-tas," Lee lamented, running a hand through his hair. "Why would he choose that hairy guy over her? I don't get it."

"Because the hairy guy got his attention," David said, reasonably. "The brunette with the ta-tas just pushed her boobs in his face like most of the other women there. I think Hank's looking for something more than some breasts, gentlemen. He needs an Omega."

Still, he was curious, too. Evan had obviously made an impression, and yet David knew that Hank had never considered a male Omega. As far as David knew, Hank was as straight as a man could come.

David looked at his watch as the credits rolled and asked, "So, who's in for tomorrow night? Same time, same place?"

Nearly everyone was in. David was supposed to have his son, Charles, with him that night, but he thought he'd probably be willing to watch the show at the station. Well, as much as Charles was willing to do *anything* that didn't entail his friends or a video game these days.

Walking out of the station, toward his car, David spared a moment to send up a prayer to whatever deity might actually exist that his best cop and his best friend would have some luck on this ridiculous television program. Because if he didn't, David didn't want to see what would happen to his friend.

+ + +

MORNING BROKE WHILE Hank was running on the beach. The territorial markers glowed in the darkness, making it clear that this was his area and his alone. The area just past the markers for about half a mile belonged to no one, and then the next set of markers would begin for another Alpha, one of the three others who were part of these televised shenanigans. Hank wondered how *they* felt about being strong-armed into this.

The heat of the sun made the air taste and feel differently; it raised the particles of water and increased the humidity against his skin. He considered shifting but decided against it. Wet fur was always a pain to deal with when he morphed. He took a deep breath and turned his face to the sun, running toward the water until he felt it rush against his feet and then turned back toward the resort.

Long strides brought him to the stairs leading up to the pool area. He paused, hands on his knees, panting lightly. The run hadn't been long enough to do anything but raise his heart rate a little, but it'd felt good to get out, away from the rustling and bustling of the resort.

He stopped now, hands on his hips, and listened, checking for movement, activity, or trouble. Not unexpectedly, the predominant noises came from the camera crews setting up, and he knew it would only be a few more moments before he was found and they'd all be on him like fleas on a dog.

Listening, though, he could tell that the Omega applicants were mostly awake. Many of them were preparing for the day. The hum of hair dryers and the rush of showers filled his ears, and then he heard a ruckus of rather distorted music thumping through a tinny set of headphones. Over it, he heard Evan Vaughn's voice saying, "Come on, Debbie, give it a listen! Can't you hear how the beat echoes the tribal drums we were listening to just last night? The connection cannot be denied! It's a thread that runs over continents and throughout history."

Hank rolled his eyes and moved on, finding nothing amiss with his territory or its people. He risked stretching his ears a little more, seeing just how far he could hear, and discovered that the barriers along the territorial markers were lined with white noise machines, effectively blocking him from eavesdropping on the other Alphas.

"Do you think he's listening to us?" a shy, Southern voice asked from the third window to the right within the resort.

"Come away from the window, Bobby, before he sees you."

"Why? Maybe I want him to see me? Maybe I want him to know I'm interested."

Hank cleared his throat and shook his head, emptying it of the chatter, and turned back to look at the ocean, letting the white-rush of it fill him up, before turning back to start what was sure to be one hell of a miserable day.

CHAPTER FOUR

T HE SECOND DAY was long.

Hank had chosen a few men in addition to Evan Vaughn in hopes of keeping things more interesting, and possibly deflecting some of the women's attention away from him and onto someone else. It hadn't seemed to work very well, though he noticed Evan holding court with a group of ladies by the pool, a box of equipment of some kind by his side, and his smile and laughter reeling them in for long periods of time.

Hank endured hours of questions and earnest eyes from various women, but he knew without a doubt that his Omega wasn't one of them. He didn't want to hurt their feelings, and yet he found himself being increasingly rude, until finally he was left alone by the towel cabana watching a huddle of women around Evan, and a small group of the guys talking by the ocean, making motions with their hands that indicated they were discussing sports.

The rest of his prospective Omegas had been scared off to their rooms, all of them having accepted that they weren't going to be chosen, and from what Hank had allowed himself to overhear, most of them were relieved.

"He's just so uptight," Bernice whispered. "I couldn't put up with that."

"Me, either," Bobby had agreed.

And it didn't even hurt a little, because Hank didn't think he could put up with any of them, either.

Evening was beginning to fall, and he'd already told the producers that he'd be having dinner in his room alone. They could have the big meal without him, because as far as he was concerned the prior two days had been a big waste of time, and he saw no reason to waste any more of it interacting with people he didn't like. He even said as much during his "confessional" period and he didn't bother trying to sound nice about it.

That night he sat in his room with the patio door open, the sounds from the pool area reached him easily. He stared into the darkness, focusing on shadows and light patterns, as he listened to Evan coaxing several female applicants into displaying their naked tits and then the ensuing laughter and splashing that occurred.

Later, after everyone but Vaughn and the girl he'd pointed out, the one called Debbie, had gone on to bed, he heard Debbie say, "I guess I just thought that it would be him out here with us, you know? Like some kind of latent adolescent fantasy of the pool party with the hot guy who is just dying to see you naked, and somehow you feel like any second someone's going to lose their bikini bottoms, and God only knows what happens next…"

"In many cultures and societies an orgy is what happens next," Evan said.

Debbie laughed and some splashing and giggling ensued before things grew quiet. Hank listened more closely, finally making out the wet, sticking sounds of kissing.

Until Evan cleared his throat. "Debbie, you're beautiful, amazing really, but—"

"But this isn't going anywhere. I know."

There was the sound of someone getting out of the pool, and then Debbie saying, "Good night, Evan. Good luck. I hope one of us ends up with an Alpha."

"Ditto, Debbie," Evan said, his tone more serious than his cheeky response implied.

"And I hope that neither of us ends up with this one," Debbie chuckled.

Evan said, "Ah, I don't know. He doesn't strike me as too bad. He's focused, sure, but he needs to be. And he's all business, I guess, but he just hasn't figured out how to loosen up, yet. That's what he needs an Omega for—to show him a little fun. You'd be good at that, don't you think?"

Debbie chuckled softly. "No, but you would. Good luck, Evan. Good night."

"Night," Evan said.

Hank could hear Debbie's footsteps padding away and the swish of the water as Evan ducked back in, humming a tune as he swam alone. His voice was strangely melodious given the high-strung tenor of it.

Hank leaned out further and listened some more, taking in the sound of Evan's heartbeat, and the way Evan's voice vibrated the surface of the water with a burbling echo. He zeroed in on the rush-woosh of Evan's blood—liquid within veins, within a body, swimming in a pool, surrounded by earth and air, and capped by atmosphere that bled into the vacuum of space.

Hank, stretching out his hearing, could almost detect where the last particles of atmosphere were held fast by gravity as the sudden absence of friction eliminated all sound. Feeling himself too far extended, Hank pulled back and looked for something close and solid to focus on, something to ground him before he tranced and spent hours or days seeking that sweet difference between sound and silence. Or shifted unexpectedly.

Evan began humming again, and his voice reached Hank easily. Hank stood up, crossed over the spongy grass the resort painstakingly planted and protected with largely-ignored signs—Please Do Not Walk On Grass—and stood, barefoot in just his pajama bottoms at the edge of the pool area.

There were no television cameras in sight, and making a quick auditory and visual sweep of the area, Hank could hear production packing up for the night. He knew that they all assumed he was in bed sleeping, having written him off as the boring Alpha almost from the beginning. Hank didn't really mind, since it meant they mainly left him alone.

Evan was swimming now, ducking under the water and popping up for gasping breaths now and again. Not the most graceful swimmer, but sturdy. Everything about Evan struck Hank as sturdy, despite his cheerful manner and endless chatting. He seemed…dependable, like a dog. A good friend, a reliable ally. Hank was certain that Evan would be chosen by one of the other Alphas. He had something about him that made a person take notice.

Hank watched him for a while, and only when Evan pulled himself out of the pool, toweled off, and started toward the resort did Hank creep back to his room.

Hank was in his bed, staring at the ceiling, and he hadn't even realized that he was listening for it, but there it was all the same. Two floors up and several rooms down, Evan Vaughn's heartbeat and then his voice, not more than a whisper, but Hank didn't need more.

"Hey, Hank," Evan said. "If you're listening, man, which I'm not saying you are, but if I were you, *I'd* be listening to everything right about now, so if you're listening, I think you'd be a great Alpha for the right person. And if they aren't in this batch, then don't give up. I'm sure she's here. You've just got to have some faith, man. Faith and…well, hell, I don't know what else, but something. It's late, but you know what I mean."

Hank did know what Evan meant, even if he didn't necessarily believe in it. He thought about his childhood and the years in between, how no one had ever really been able to reach him and wondered if something as loose as faith would get him through. Or if he'd have to resign his post, give up being a cop, and accept a gruesome end for himself. Because he couldn't imagine anchoring his life to someone like Debbie. Or Markie. Or Shawn. Or Joe. Or any of the others he'd talked to today.

He turned over in the bed and listened as Evan's footsteps moved through the hotel room, focused on Evan's breathing, and startled when Evan's whisper sounded so loud that it could have come from right next to him. "Uh, Hank? I'm gonna beat off now, so, if you're listening, could you…you know? Stop?"

Hank blushed, as though he'd been caught out as a Peeping Tom. He cleared his throat, stood up, and rubbed his hands together, staring out the doorway to his patio, gazing at the ocean in the distance, deliberately *not* listening to Evan's breathing speeding up, or his heart pounding in his chest, or the slap of Evan's hand on his own cock.

Hank rubbed his eyes and coughed. Dammit…he *was* listening. He glanced around the room, his eyes landing on the white noise generator next to his bed, and he turned it on.

The instant reprieve was good. Right. Necessary, even.

Hank sat down on his bed, elbows on his knees, face in his hands, gazing down at the tent in his pajama bottoms, wanting to take it in hand and do *something* about it, but he knew better.

Not now. He'd have to wait.

It was too risky, riskier than indulging himself by focusing on the edge of the atmosphere, and, besides, he didn't have any good fantasy material anyway. There wasn't a single woman in the last two days that he'd want to get naked with anyway. Why was his cock acting up *now*?

Must've been Evan and Debbie talking about orgies, and the pheromones Evan was putting off during his jerk-off, which Hank could still smell if he tried.

But he wasn't trying. Not *trying*.

Hank consciously pulled in his sense of smell, hoping that he wouldn't need to rub a tiny bit of camphor under his nose to keep from smelling something he had no business smelling. Hank rolled his eyes and sighed. The last thing he needed was vicarious erections.

He used the fancy sink in the ridiculous A-list bathroom, complete with a gold-plated phone by the bath, to splash cold water on his face to cool down. And then, when he thought his dick had the idea, and it was safe, he pulled his sleep mask down and pushed his sense of hearing into the white noise, soaking it up as he drifted to sleep.

HE WAS A bear. It was raining, but he could see his den ahead. He had to guard it, protect it from someone or something that was trying to get inside. He could feel them all around him, eyes in the darkness, pushing closer and closer to the den where his family lived. And then he saw it. The wolf. It was instantaneous, no time for thought. He launched at it. The wolf turned onto its back, belly up, eyes open wide. He approached cautiously, and when he placed his paw on the wolf's vulnerable stomach, the wolf closed his eyes.

CHAPTER FIVE

H ANK WOKE UP, punched his pillow, and stared out the window at the star-filled sky. The clock told him it was five-thirty in the morning, and he considered pulling on his running shorts, but opted for a robe over his pajama bottoms instead. He used the in-room coffee machine and took his cup out onto the patio, but the surf called to him, so he walked directly toward it, through the scrub, not bothering with the path. The ocean was dark and vast, and the break of day was visible to his eyes only as a long line glimmering at the horizon.

"Nice, isn't it?" The voice was cheerful, though still sleepy.

Hank nodded.

Just like in the bathroom the other night, it wasn't as if he hadn't known that Evan was there on the beach, too, walking along the edge of the scrub and the sand. It was just that it didn't bother him or register as a disturbance.

Well, not until Evan spoke, and then Hank grimaced and swallowed his coffee. "A little early for chit-chat," Hank grumbled, crossing an arm over his torso and staring into the distance.

"Sure," Evan said. "But isn't it always?"

Hank grunted in reply and took another swig of coffee.

Evan was silent only for a moment, though. "Man, I had weird dreams last night. Do you ever have weird dreams?"

Hank gave him a look. It wasn't so much that he wanted Evan to go away as that he wanted Evan to shut up. There really was no need to talk this early in the morning.

About anything.

Much less about weird dreams.

"I do," Evan said. "I have weird dreams a lot. Sometimes, I dream that I'm not even an Omega or a human. How wild is that?" Evan chuckled. As he went on talking, his hands moved with his words, as though carefully laying out his thoughts before they flew away from him. "Of course, that probably happens to you all the time. Dreaming that you're in your animal form, I mean. But as an Omega, I don't shift. I serve as the mated touchstone for a shifter to return to. But, in some cultures, they believe that when you dream that you're a specific animal it's your totem speaking to you. Your symbol animal, you know? Like your spiritual Omega…even if you're a human or an Omega. It's confusing. But it's like your dream animal is your own Omega. It can show you the way."

"Tell that to my supervisors," Hank muttered.

"What?"

"I said, tell that…never mind."

"Oh." Evan ran his hand through his unruly hair, pushing the length of it behind his ears. "I get you. You're talking about being your own Omega, right? Or not needing one? If *you* have a symbol animal that isn't you—in shifter or human form—that's totally wild. But it isn't really the same, Hank, because the concept of a symbol animal is more about directing you to what *you* need, and an Omega is more about keeping you alive. There's a critical difference there—"

"Captain," Hank said.

"Yeah?"

"Shut up."

Evan cleared his throat and then laughed a little. "Right. Early yet. Too early for chit-chat." But as though he could only keep his tongue still for a few seconds at a time, he began again.

"So, tonight you choose the person you're going to have a one-on-one date with; pretty exciting stuff, huh?"

Hank said, "Have you suddenly turned into Warren now? 'How do you feel, Alpha Morrow? Must be great to have all these groupies for no reason at all, huh?'"

Evan laughed again. "Yeah, man. Sucks to be you. I'm just writhing with pain on your behalf over here, let me tell you." Evan pushed his hair from his face again and then said, "Well, seriously, though, what about it? Do you have someone in mind?"

Hank let out a long breath and shook his head.

"Yeah, even though the idea of all these people lining up to be at *my* beck and call doesn't seem all bad, I can't say I blame you. No one here really floats my boat either, man."

"Sycophants," Hank muttered.

"I was gonna go with 'boring,' but, yeah, you said it," Evan agreed. "Well, you'll find a way to endure an evening, I'm sure."

Hank wasn't.

Evan went on, "Anyway, tomorrow, in the morning, I leave for the next Alpha camp. I think it's Cameron's, though it might be Heather's. I don't think it's Fong's yet, though. He's next week sometime. Warren told me."

Hank gripped his coffee mug more tightly and took a drink, saying nothing.

"Yeah, so I'm kind of excited, you know? I mean, who knows what lies ahead, but I've just got a good feeling. Women tend to like me, if you know what I mean." Evan made a motion with his hand, and Hank cleared his throat again and looked away. Evan seemed a little embarrassed. "Well, I'm a people person, really. People like me."

"Are you sure about that?" Hank asked.

Evan laughed and bumped Hank's shoulder. "Oh, come on.

You saw the way the women respond to me, didn't you? I kept them away from you yesterday anyway. Don't I even get a thank you for that?"

Hank smirked. "Yeah, sure. Thanks, Captain. Good work seducing the other applicants."

"You're welcome—and, hey, wait a minute there, I didn't *seduce* anyone. Well, okay, maybe a little, but they all enjoyed the seduction. It was welcome. If you know what I mean."

Hank chuckled and shook his head. "You're something else, Evan Vaughn."

"That's what the girls always tell me," Evan said, pumping his fist and making an "uh-uh" sound.

Hank snorted, shook his head, and smiled around his coffee cup as he stared out at the ocean. He took a deep breath and sorted through the odors. Salt, sand, sea. Coffee, toothpaste, the odd scent of 'scentless' shampoo. Sweat, warm skin, exhaled breath. Calming. Centering. Hank liked it. Hell, Hank liked Evan.

Maybe he'd have the one-on-one date with *him* tonight. At least they both knew where they stood.

Evan moved in front of Hank, his eyes earnest, but not in the fake way that everyone else seemed to look at him. "Yeah, well, wish me luck, okay? I'd like to get chosen by someone, and I think my best hope lies with the ladies. I'll leave you alone now."

Hank sipped his coffee and said, "What's the rush? Got somewhere to be?"

Evan smiled and said, "No rush, man. No rush."

Hank cleared his throat and asked, "So that's your preference?"

"Huh?"

"Women are your preference?"

"What? Oh, sure. I mean, I guess so. I've been with a few

men in my time and it's just…different, you know?"

Hank didn't know. Well, not since he was about ten years old, but that had been kid-stuff, just experimentation, nothing real. Nothing important.

Evan went on, "Not bad. More…primal. So, you know, if Fong decided I was the one for him, I could live with it." Evan grinned wickedly. "Oh, hell yeah, have you seen him? Incredible, man. Just incredible. Strong arms, big legs—being held down by him…?" Evan seemed to drift off on that thought. Then he cleared his throat and said, "So, yeah, I could live with it."

Hank shifted, his stomach lurching. Too much coffee. He dumped it out into the sand beside him, watching as it soaked in, avoiding Evan's eyes.

But Evan kept talking, "But, yes, all in all, I tend to be with women. I like their softness, and there's never anything bad to say about a nice pair of…you know? Am I right? Besides, women seem to think I'm adorable."

Hank scoffed. "Ah, maybe that's what those women were saying about you when I thought they were calling you a dork."

"Oh, yeah? Is that what they were saying?" Evan said, sarcastically, bumping against Hank's arm with his shoulder.

Hank shrugged and sat down in the sand, digging his feet in. Evan didn't hesitate to follow him down. Hank watched as Evan pushed his hair out of his face again.

"Where did I put that hair band? I swear, Hank, it's the world's biggest mystery outside of where the socks disappear to…where do the hair bands *go*?"

"I understand that Bon Jovi is still making a good living and kicking up their heels in New Jersey in between tours."

"Haha, man, hilarious," Evan said mildly, giving up searching his jeans pockets for the band and just letting his hair fly wild in the morning wind off the ocean.

They sat together in silence for a few peaceful minutes until Hank said, "So, good luck then."

"Yeah, for sure," Evan agreed. He patted Hank's knee and stood up, stretching, the lift of his T-shirt revealing a length of dark hair between his navel and the top of his jeans. "Later, man."

Hank listened to the sound of Evan walking away, the pattern of his footfalls, and the creaking of his joints. Hank closed his eyes as the sun peeped over the line of the horizon, bright and overwhelming.

He took a deep breath and mixed in with the scent of the sea and the salt and the sand was a touch of Evan's sweat and warm skin, and it centered him, filling him with a sense of peace.

Until he heard the television crew commenting, "Yeah, got that whole thing. Gonna be hard to edit it so that it's appropriate for a family program, though."

Another voice, this one with a British accent, said, "Yeah, that Vaughn guy. He's a cheeky one."

Hank didn't turn around, didn't look. As much as it made him feel trapped to have his every move recorded, it was part of what he'd been signed up for, and unless he wanted to just quit, go home to suffer it out, and to put his co-workers and friends through hell with him, then he'd have to deal.

At least for now.

Maybe if something got serious with someone, then he'd have to put his foot down…on someone's throat.

For now, it was just Evan they recording his interactions with, and that felt safe. That was okay.

DAVID AND THE rest of the police department were less surprised than Evan looked when Hank chose Evan to have the first one-on-one date.

"I knew it," one of the guys from Homicide said. "Morrow's a fag."

"Explains a lot," a woman's voice called out, but David didn't see who it was.

"Shut it," David said, glaring at the guy's captain, demanding with his eyes that he be taken in hand. "An Omega is not a lover in the traditional sense. It's about a soul connection, not a genital connection."

"Right, and Morrow's soul is a fag."

The captain from Homicide took control before David had to kick some ass himself, but the room felt tense after the slur.

"Everybody calm down," Ben, one of Hank's friends and fellow officers, said. David was glad he hadn't gone over to beat the snot out of the offending officer from the other department. "It's just the first set of fifteen. He's just choosing someone that he doesn't want to kill. You know how Hank is. He probably doesn't like any of them."

David agreed, but there was something about Evan Vaughn that kept Hank's interest. *That* even David could see.

As it was, the host, Warren, was referring to the two of them as the Odd Couple, noting that Evan had called Hank by his first name from the very beginning, and that Hank hadn't even flinched. Warren went on, "It'll be interesting to see how Hank reacts to Evan going to the other Alphas' camps. One of the first traditional signs of an intent to bond is territorial behavior from the Alpha toward the prospective Omega. So far, it appears that Morrow is exhibiting this behavior completely unbeknownst to himself. Watch this clip of him smiling at one of Vaughn's more comic comments—despite being several rooms away...."

After the clip aired, complete with time stamps at the bottom of the screen to show that the smile directly followed Evan's joke, and to indicate that the prospective Omega, Markie, with whom Hank was actually holding a conversation with, had not said anything worthy of such a stunning grin, Warren continued, "And yet Morrow seems unaware that he's monitoring Vaughn covertly, or of any of his other behaviors. What does that mean for both of them? Tune in tomorrow to see what happens during tonight's one-on-one date."

David sighed, glanced around the room at the mixed-up expressions on his colleagues' faces. He didn't know if sending Hank to this television program had been such a good idea. Demystifying the Alpha not only to the world, but in front of his men, didn't seem like a good idea to David.

Then again, it hadn't been David's call.

And Hank was running out of time. There were only a few years left at the most before Hank was lost to his Alpha senses and grew unable to control his shifting. Some had suggested that Hank, because of the years he'd spent repressing his Alpha gifts as a child, might have less than that.

Unless an Omega was found.

So, really, what other choice had they had? Seeing Hank fail on the job and lose lives? Watching him eventually suffer from not only the guilt of that, but the loss of control? Seeing him eventually shut down entirely, trapped in a world of sensory overload, and even, quite possibly, die?

David cleared his throat and ordered everyone from the room. He didn't ask who would be back the following night. In fact, he took another route entirely. "From now on, if you want to watch it, watch it on your own time. In your own homes." What had seemed like a good opportunity for camaraderie now felt dangerous and a breeding ground for trouble. "I don't want to see you here. Any of you. Got that?"

Tense looks flew around, and David didn't really care. He glanced up at the screen again. He felt like he'd just watched Hank masturbating or picking his nose. It was one thing to see a man like Fong actively searching for an Omega, and it was another thing to watch his private friend, Hank, revealing intimate truths about himself for the whole world to see.

Secret truths that even Hank didn't know.

"Come on, Charles," David said, pulling his teenage son up by the arm. "Time to get you back to your mom's. She'll say I had you out too late as it is."

Charles jerked his arm away and glared around the room. "I don't see what their problem is," Charles said.

"Who?" David asked.

"Them," Charles said, nodding toward the men who were still muttering words like 'fag' under their breath. "It's not like he's asking *them* to suck his cock."

David choked back a laugh, covering his mouth so that Charles wouldn't see. "Come *on*, boy. I've got to get you home. Stop dilly-dallying around and get a damn move on."

Charles rolled his eyes. "Yes, sir, Dad, sir, Captain Washington, *sir*."

"And enough lip from you," David said, escorting him out the door, proud and pleased that his kid, at least, wasn't a bigot.

CHAPTER SIX

"**W**ELL, IF THIS isn't the most romantic thing I've ever seen," Evan said, sarcasm and laughter mixing his voice into a higher pitch than usual.

Hank turned from studying the line of colors from the sun setting on the horizon and lifted his water-filled champagne glass in a toast, and said, "And it's all for you, Captain."

Evan laughed, walking closer to Hank, hands stuffed into his suit pockets, his tie a bit askew, and his hair loose in the wind. "Yeah, me…or whoever you'd chosen for tonight."

Hank smiled, a small laugh caught in his throat. "Well, you know how it is—it's all the same, a little roses and a little champagne will have any potential Omega—"

"On their back with their legs in the air?"

"Shh, it's a family show, Captain," Hank said.

Evan nodded and lifted his brows excitedly. "Yeah, a family show. Such great values here. Prostitute yourself for a chance at your dream."

Hank cleared his throat and looked away. "Is that how you see it? Is that how you feel about what you're doing?"

Evan backpedaled quickly. "Whoa, whoa, slow down there, Hank. I was poking fun, trying to keep it light; you know how it is. Things get intense here, and I…."

Hank turned to face Evan again, his eyes sweeping over to the table placed atop the massive black lava rock they were standing on, which had required four sets of stairs welded to the side to reach.

The table was covered in roses and rose petals, the food served beneath shining covered platters. There was champagne for Evan and bottled water for Hank, and the sun set vibrantly on the horizon of the crashing ocean. It was romantic, it was beautiful, and, ultimately, it did feel like prostitution.

Hank was okay with that for himself. It was part of the deal, but to think that Evan felt that way—it unnerved him, made him feel unsteady, as though the rock were shifting beneath him.

"Do you, Evan?"

Evan's eyes were on his face, studying it, serious and nervous, too. "Truth?"

Hank snorted. "Yeah, truth."

"Well, no and yes. I'm here of my own volition. I'm aware of the games they play, and that it's all fake in a way, but I know that I'm also looking for something real."

Hank crossed his arms over his chest, unconvinced.

"Yeah, yeah, I know that's what they all say on those stupid reality shows, and I know that this *is* one of those stupid reality shows, but…"

Evan stepped up to his side, his pulse beating faster and his eyes dilating. Hank took in these changes and wanted to calm him, but he didn't know how.

Evan laughed, but it sounded strained. "I don't know, Hank, man, all right? I just know that I wanted to do this, and here we are, and look!" Evan's grin cracked wide, and it was real. Something unwound inside Hank, and he felt his shoulders relax. "Champagne for me, water for you, a lovely view…and we're friends, right? Or starting to be? So, why waste it? I know you didn't choose me for any reason other than that you don't want to punch me—very much. So, no worries there, man." Evan reached out and stroked Hank's arm.

He sucked in a strangled breath.

Evan's smile turned soothing. "Just take some deep breaths. See this for what it is, and let it go. Let it go…that's it. In and out, and have a drink of water, too, while you're at it. It's good for the mind *and* body. Hydration is very important in life, in more ways than anyone really—"

"Captain?"

"Yeah?"

"Shut up."

"Right. And you're breathing now anyway. And drinking. Good job."

Hank glanced at the cameras that had been rigged along the perimeter of the stone, recording everything about their interactions. He could feel them, hear them, smell them all the time. They were everywhere but in his room, which he'd insisted on as an important exception, and the producers allowed the privacy when he'd pushed. Still, he forgot them sometimes. He had to or he'd risk losing it like a caged animal.

"So, what's for dinner?" Evan asked, rubbing his hands together. "I'm famished."

"Hope you're not a vegetarian," Hank said.

"Nope, bring it on."

Several hours later, Hank sat with a pretty intoxicated Evan in the giant beanbag chair that'd been placed on the rock for them to relax on after dinner. At first, they'd talked about Evan's experience at the Omega program at Spruce University. It was a good program, one of the best in the country, and it took a very talented Omega candidate to gain entry to it.

"All Omega candidates have the natural ability to bring Alphas out of a trance and to form a bond," Evan said. "Just like with Alphas, it is presumed to be genetic, but they still haven't discovered what combination of genes makes that happen. Some of us, though, seem to have stronger abilities, and that's part of the testing that you have to go through before you can even get into any program, much less a program of Spruce's quality."

Hank knew, though, that it took more than that to attend Spruce University. Evan was exceptionally intelligent—Hank could tell that from simply being around him—but he would have had to pass some incredibly difficult exams with flying colors to be admitted to the Spruce program.

"I started studying for it when I was sixteen," Evan said, taking another sip of wine. "When I was kid, I'd stolen a microscope—yes, Hank, I was a science nerd, okay?—and the cop who talked to me just happened to be an Alpha, and he touched my arm during the lecture about how it was bad to steal, and he was like… whoa, you know? Just totally shocked. He said he'd never felt a stronger Omega, not even his own, and he's the one who got me started on this path."

Hank rubbed a hand over his eyes, confused by the weird feeling in his stomach. He didn't like the idea of the cop in Evan's story being the first to sense Evan's Omeganess.

"And that was that. He was like, 'If you become a bonded Omega, you can have as many microscopes as you want. I promise you that.' And I was, like, 'Cool,' but when I started studying tribes and their Alphas, that all faded away. I couldn't stop learning. I was absolutely starved for it, man. And that's when I knew what it meant to be predestined for something—or someone."

Hank felt Evan slump against him a bit. He wondered if he should move, or make the kid sit up, but he didn't. "You'll make a great Omega for an Alpha, Captain."

Evan's smile, and the way he tucked his hair behind his ear tugged at Hank's heart. He wanted to protect that motion, that expression, and he understood completely why the Alpha who'd met Evan as a kid had encouraged him.

Somehow, a little later, they started talking about Evan's old lovers, and he began comparing the technique of one girl to another, adding, "I showed my last girlfriend my journals, man, 'cause I thought she'd appreciate the honesty, you know?"

"You mean, you hoped she'd learn a thing or two?" Hank countered.

"Well, maybe, it wasn't a conscious thought, but, yeah, maybe."

"Just how detailed were these journals, Captain?"

"Hank, I'm an anthropologist."

Hank chuckled, sipping his water, enjoying the wind in his hair and the scent of saltwater. "Detailed, then."

"Yep."

Hank smiled and shook his head, his arm going around Evan's shoulders and shaking him. "You're supposed to burn the evidence; don't you know that? When I got married, I burned all the old letters from the old girlfriends."

"A purification ritual—"

"No, just an offensive tactic."

Evan shifted out from under his arm and sat up a little straighter. His face was red from laughing and talking, and probably from drinking, too, but he looked pretty charming with his expression all serious and innocent in a strange way. Hank had never seen someone look at another person with such open, trusting eyes. "You had a wife, Hank?" Evan asked.

Hank swallowed and looked away from the supposed windows to Evan's soul, and he shrugged. "Yeah, didn't last. I wasn't…. It didn't work out."

Evan nodded, leaning back against the beanbag chair, turning his eyes up to the sky. Hank glanced up at the star-filled night, too, and tried to follow a line of light from each star, and he wanted to laugh a little when it seemed that each one directed his eyes back to Evan's face. He wondered if someone had spiked his water, because he was feeling strangely jovial, loose, and easy. Kind of high.

"It's hard…when it's not an Omega," Evan said, softly.

Hank nodded, closing his eyes as he thought of Valerie. He tried not to think of her too often. The sense of shame, the overwhelming failure of it all, made him feel too much, and it was hard to deal with his emotions when they came on that strong. They nearly swamped him and broke him out of reality. Once, unable to endure the pain, he'd shifted and run into the woods in his bear form and remained there a week.

Another reason he needed an Omega.

"You loved her," Evan said, stating it as fact.

"Yes. I did. But love isn't everything," Hank said.

"Was she blonde?"

"Kind of blonde," Hank said, smiling at the memory of Valerie's trips to the hairdresser to get her dishwater hair made lighter.

"Leggy?"

"Definitely leggy." Hank thought of her legs a mile long, the way they'd parted to let him in, and he shook his head a little to get rid of the image.

"Was it the sex?" Evan asked.

Hank blinked. "What?"

"It's just that all the research indicates that an Alpha without an Omega often has trouble with sex."

"No, that wasn't the problem," Hank said, suddenly acutely aware of the cameras posted all around and wanting to drop through the massive ton of rock beneath him.

Evan was still talking. "There was this one guy, right? An Alpha back in the old days before we knew a lot, and he kind of blew the curve. See, all Alphas are inherently bisexual, because, you know, the right Omega can come in any kind of package, and an Alpha has to be able to bond with the Omega when presented in whatever form."

"Yeah," Hank said, though his tongue felt dry and heavy. He sipped more water.

"You already know this, Hank. I'm not telling you anything new. After all, you spent two years with the White Moon people, right? And they think that Omegas are reincarnated from life to life, and that when one Omega dies, he passes directly to another where his spirit is reborn, and on and on. They think it's true of Alphas, too, and so there could occasionally be massive age differences to work around, and there was also the issue of how to deal with their culture's unfortunate bias against homosexuality in general, but the Alpha and Omega could be exceptions to the rule—"

Hank let Evan babble on because at least he wasn't asking Hank about sex with Valerie anymore, at least he'd left that behind. Hank cleared his throat, half-listening, so the words "inherently bisexual" hit him way too late in the game to dispute. But the next thing Evan said caused him to do a double take.

"But this one guy, a big honcho high up in the military, back in the day when the sexual aspect of the Omega and Alpha relationship was still not completely understood—well, not that it is *completely* understood now, of course, because there is still plenty of confusion—but, anyway, this guy was married, right? Had a wife, and he was crazy about her. I met her later, did some interviews with her, and she's a lovely lady, old now and everything, and probably watching this show," Evan waved absently as though saying hi to her. "But, yeah, so everyone thought that this Alpha's male Omega was just…you know helpful on the job, kept the Alpha focused in battles and stuff.

But after his death, the Omega and the wife came out and admitted that they'd been involved in a sexual and romantic vee triad the whole time!"

Hank's eyes darted from Evan's knee, to his blabbering mouth, to the edge of the rock dropping off into the darkness, and back again. "A vee triad?"

Of all the things to say, Hank didn't know why that was what came out. How about 'Enough,' or 'Shut up,' or 'I don't want to hear it,' or any number of things to make this humiliating conversation stop?

"Yeah, the wife and the Omega focused on the Alpha…sexually, you know?" Evan made a V-shape with his hands. "See, the Alpha was the pivot point, the focus. He was really possessive, territorial as all Alphas are, and couldn't handle either of them touching each other, but the only way he could perform with his wife was with his Omega's help. That's how it started apparently—just the Omega helping him not to trance during sex, helping him to perform, and then it went from there to the Alpha getting it on with both of them together, at the same time."

"What?" Hank said, standing up quickly, almost jumping back from Evan, who looked confused.

"Yeah, man, what's the problem? Everyone benefited from it. The bonded Omega and Alpha got what they needed from each other, and the wife got her needs met, which saved their marriage. It was all good in the end. After the Alpha's death, the Omega and the wife lived on together as friends."

"What?"

Evan made the V-shape again and said, kind of chuckling, "You know, a vee."

Hank took a step back with half-clenched fists. "Listen, Captain, I'm not bisexual."

"Well, actually—"

"I'm not bisexual," Hank reiterated. "And it wasn't sex that ended my marriage. It's not easy being married to an Alpha. That's what ended my marriage. That and nothing else."

Evan's hands came up in surrender. "Of course, man. Sure. Whatever you say."

The lack of conviction in Evan's voice irritated him, and fur bristled beneath his skin. Hank took a moment to keep himself in line. "Look, forget it. Let's just call it a night."

Evan's eyes darted away, hurt. "Sure thing. Sorry, man. I, uh, didn't mean to push your buttons. I just…yeah."

Hank's chest ached.

Evan swallowed hard, nodded, and stood up, too. His tie was long gone, having fluttered off into the breeze over the rock when he'd taken it off. Chest hair tufted where his shirt was unbuttoned at the top, his pulse beating rapidly there, and his heart pounded loud and hard. Evan was scared. Of what? Of him?

Hank took a deep breath, turned as though to go, but for some reason he paused long enough to catch Evan's eye and say, "Good luck with the next Alpha, Captain."

Evan's expression of vulnerability cut through Hank's anger as he said, "Sure. You, too."

"Do you need help getting down from here?"

Evan was drunk after all. That was probably why he'd said those things about Hank's marriage and sex life; it couldn't have been anything more. He couldn't have *known*.

"Nah, man. I'm okay. You go on. I'm just gonna sit here a while and…admire the sunrise."

Hank glanced toward the jungle. Yes, there on the opposite horizon, a small glimmer. They'd been here all night. It didn't seem like that much time had passed, but he supposed it had.

After all, Evan had told him endless stories about growing up with a hippie for a mother, and the literally hundreds of women that he'd dated, and Hank had soaked it up, taken it in like he was starved for it.

Hank studied Evan's form sinking down into the beanbag chair, his normally clear and open eyes now gazing glumly toward the horizon, not looking at Hank at all.

"Listen, Captain," Hank started. "I'm sorry. You're a good kid, okay?"

"It's all right, Hank. Sometimes I talk too much. It's a problem of mine. You'd think I'd learn." Evan cleared his throat and went on, "I'm not a kid, you know. Thirty and counting. Definitely not a kid."

Hank wanted to comfort him, but the flash of embarrassment at the thought of the cameras recording everything shot through him, and he glanced around, torn between wanting to make Evan feel better and wanting to get back to his room.

Still, Hank took some pity and said, "You're young, though. There's time."

"Yeah," Evan said softly. "Letting you go with love, man. Thanks."

"Huh?"

"Just something my mom says. Listen, Hank. I'm leaving for the next camp in a few hours. So, hey, I just want you to know that I've liked knowing you. If nothing else, maybe after this is all over we can be friends."

"I'd like that."

Evan smiled. "Me, too."

Hank turned his back then, glancing over his shoulder only once at the image of Evan huddled down into the bean bag chair, his hair in the wind, and his breathing shallow and off-rhythm.

Hank took the stairs slowly, thinking of Evan's offer of friendship, imagining a day when this mess was all over, thinking of meeting Evan for dinner and laughing over food.

But what of his own Omega? Would she like that? And what if Evan was chosen by another Alpha? Territory issues would preclude any friendship between them, then.

Evan knew that.

Hank sighed, a deep sorrow filling him at the thought that he might not see Evan any more after all of this was over.

To be honest, it wasn't often that Hank met someone he wanted to call a friend.

CHAPTER SEVEN

THE NEXT GROUP of thirty-five applicants arrived, and they weren't much better. Having learned from experience, though, Hank kept a small pad on him during the introduction evening and made notes to trigger his memory when it came time to choose. There was no one, though, that caught his interest, and despite being able to call out names easily and quickly, it was just as random and meaningless as the first time had been.

For the next several days, he went to bed early every night, declining even to choose a person for a one-on-one date, which caused a great deal of hurt feelings, but Hank couldn't imagine meeting one of these Omegas on that huge black rock where he'd been with Evan. He couldn't force himself through the motions of a date together. Somehow it felt like it would be tainting something, insulting Evan, or reducing him to just one of the many Omega groupies that Hank could barely tolerate.

The next group wasn't much better, though there was an older woman, Cindy, who reminded him of Jenny, the maid who had basically raised him and his brother, Randall. She'd been the only one in the house to show him much affection. And then his parents had seen her deported when they discovered she was in the country illegally.

Hank spent most of his time with Cindy, asking about her life in the Philippines, though never talking to her much about Jenny; those were his private memories, painful and raw even now, and he didn't share them with many people, much less a complete stranger.

Cindy was his choice for the one-on-one date, too. She was charming and wonderful, though completely aware that the connection between them was pure nostalgia on Hank's part, and that he wasn't interested in her as an Omega. Once it was over, Hank realized after a few days that he couldn't even remember her name. He just knew that she wasn't Jenny.

As the weeks passed, Hank began having even more odd dreams. It'd come to the point where he nearly dreaded sleep, because he knew he'd wake up a few hours later, drenched in sweat and exhausted.

There was the usual dream, the one with the bear and the wolf; it was the same dream he'd had off and on for nearly a decade. But, in addition to that, after Evan's lewd allusion to the vee triad, he'd begun having dreams of Valerie again.

In his sleep, he twisted in the sheets to images of her legs spread, her arms open, receiving him, taking him in. And in his dreams there was always a voice-over, familiar and soothing: Evan saying, "Breathe in and out, let her go with love, hydration is important, man, that's good, lots of B names, by the way, and that's it, Hank, just like that…"

He'd wake so hard that he wanted to cry, and he'd have to take cold showers to cool off, to come down from unwanted arousal.

Evan had been right; it was sex that had ended his marriage. He couldn't make love to Valerie without feeling the urge to shift and then overcompensating by leaning into the sensations and disappearing into a trance. He hadn't been able to manage sex with her from the beginning, not without disappearing into the sensation, sometimes for hours, and once for over a day.

The last time, he'd come out of the trance with Valerie still under him, her breathing shallow from his weight, and her eyes distant and glazed. Trapped. He'd been too heavy to move and she'd been trapped under him for over two hours. She could have died.

She said she understood, she said she wasn't angry, but after that they'd never had sex again. Not even with Valerie on top. She was just too far away from him. Not that he'd ever been good at letting her in. No, he'd never been good at that part of the marriage, either.

As for his status as one of the stars of this bizarre reality show, every day Hank thought about calling the whole thing off. He hadn't met anyone who could possibly be his Omega, and he was starting to feel horrified, even humiliated, that he would have gone through all of this—prostituted himself in front of the camera, his pals at the station, in front of God's whole earth—only to get no pay off. Only to go home and eventually lose control of his senses, lose control of himself, and someday enter an endless trance and die or shift into an animal permanently.

He felt hopeless and angry when the fourth and final set of thirty-five applicants arrived. Among them was a young woman named Allison.

Hank couldn't say what it was about her, but she made his heart skip a beat, and his cock feel heavy. He couldn't concentrate when she talked, and he found himself thinking only of her pussy, wondering how it would taste when wet with lust, and how it would feel wrapped around his cock. Her voice was like dripping honey, slow and golden, and he felt drugged and thick in her presence.

It was terrifying. Like time stood still when he was with her. Intoxicating. Breathless. Hot. Hank had a hard time finding more words than that to describe it. His mind simply shut down the moment he got near her.

The feeling she evoked was so strong in him that he didn't

even ask her for the one-on-one date, afraid that he'd end up between her legs on that bean bag chair showing the world his face in ecstasy, bonding with her before he'd even decided if she could truly support him in the middle of a stand-off or help him stay focused during an investigation. Making him want nothing more than to fuck did not a good Omega make, not even close.

So, he asked another woman, Jane, who was quiet and nerdy and didn't say much, to spend the evening with him on the big, black rock. He felt guilty about it off and on all night, because while Jane lurched from one topic to another, attempting to make a connection, Hank found himself sniffing the air, looking for Allison's scent, and when he'd managed to catch the soft strain of it, he could swear he tasted her on his lips.

Knowing it was going nowhere, Jane excused herself early, and Hank was relieved. He sat on the rock staring out at the ocean for hours. He left before dawn, though, walking the line of the beach and water, still in his suit and trailed by cameras. He was hot, itchy, and overwhelmed.

And when he wasn't thinking of Allison and the strange way she made him feel, he was wishing that Evan was around to talk to about this, to see what he'd say, because even if it was useless information or biased opinions, Evan would have *something* to say about Allison, and then Hank wouldn't be alone, drowning in this mad lust.

The next morning, before he was dressed, a knock came at his door. It was Allison, standing there speaking in words that couldn't seem to penetrate his suddenly lust-fogged brain. She wore a sundress printed with fruit and flowers, and a flirtatious smile. Hank opened the door wider, taking her into his room; his hands shook as he closed and locked the door behind him, shutting it in the face of the camera crew, shutting it before he could change his mind.

He kissed her then, wet and soft, and slippery smooth. He groaned into her mouth and pushed her onto the bed, bringing his thigh up. He pulled her against him, humping hard and mindless, moaning when her small frame pushed up against his larger one. She shoved her hands under his shirt, her fingertips electric on his nipples, and he caught on the sensation. Tripping on that wire of lust again, falling into the whole of it, shivering, hanging, trapped in a buzzing, endless field of touch.

He came out of it with Allison still under him, her voice small and scared, and streams of tears running down her face. He pulled back, shaking and still hard, so hard that he felt like he couldn't breathe, but he had to stop. This wasn't right. Her voice…her voice…it didn't ground him but just sent him flying, and he put his hand over her mouth.

"Shh, shhh, shhh sweetheart," he begged. "Don't cry. Just…go. Go now. Please."

She did. Hank knew that she did because her flip-flops slapped softly across the floor, the door opened, and a burst of activity rushed into the room. He heard the questions and her voice, soft and still wet with tears, responding with a flippant tone.

Hank shook like a leaf, fear roiling in his stomach, and lust still rushing through his veins. He collapsed on the bed, exhausted from the brief trance, and stayed there motionless, afraid to even move.

Hours later he woke to the sound of pounding on his door. The producers were worried, they'd sent doctors, but Hank waved them off.

He showered, washing the scent of Allison off of his skin, and then studied himself in the mirror. It'd been a close call. Had they…no, had he…they could be bonded now.

Hank frowned.

It was off, though. Something had gone wrong.

She was an Omega. Hank shouldn't have tranced with her there to hold him back. Even if she wasn't his Omega, she was *an Omega.*

Unless…he'd heard stories that sometimes once an Alpha had begun a bond…no other Omega could reach him until the bond was completed.

But, no, that was impossible.

Hank closed his eyes, bowed his head. He could taste her on his tongue. She was like apples in fall. He could lose himself in the flesh of her. He almost had.

And that wasn't a good thing, not when he didn't have a way back.

CHAPTER EIGHT

E VAN RETURNED THE next morning, and there was a weird rush of confusion when Hank saw him standing in the lobby of the resort.

Evan's hair was in a ponytail, and his lips were pushed forward in a thoughtful and frustrated pout as he stared down at his bags.

Hank felt divided. He could walk across the room to Allison as he'd planned, apologize to her, and see if she wanted to try again or if it was just another lost cause. Or, he could stop and greet Evan, ask him what was wrong and why he had that dissatisfied look on his face.

He hesitated, glancing at Allison by the door to the resort's bar, her blonde hair twisted up in a complicated braid and her bust highlighted in a shirt that left little to his imagination.

He flushed all over with renewed lust. He took a step in her direction, but something caught his attention, and he turned his head, zeroing in on Evan shuffling through a bag and muttering under his breath about his mp3 player.

Hank realized he'd chosen Evan over Allison only when he knelt beside him and asked, "Missing something, Captain?"

"Yeah, my mp3 player." Evan's hands lifted and fell in ongoing animation as he went on, "I left it behind somewhere, and I don't even know where. I had it last night by the pool at Fong's resort, and, oh, man, Hank, you should see that place. You got totally robbed, because Fong's resort is just so *cool*."

Hank lifted a brow, not sure how he felt about his current territory being disparaged.

Evan rocked back on his heels, his hands moving to indicate the size and shape of things. "They have a giant swimming area with dolphins, which, yeah, has some pretty serious ethical issues attached, but opportunity is still opportunity, man, and, well, Fong chose three of us to go in with him, and, *Hank*. It was so cool! Amazing! I felt like I was communicating with them, and they made these amazing little noises!" Evan attempted an imitation. "I'd love to tell my mother about it, but I think she'd probably call PETA on me. Hank, have you ever touched a dolphin? They're so soft and—wait, wait! Yes, I had it by the dolphin pool this morning before we left. I was curious to see if they would like Kate Bush." Evan laughed a little and looked mildly embarrassed. "I mean, yeah, there is some incidental evidence that animals might have musical preferences, but—"

Hank attempted to get Evan back on track. "Captain, your mp3 player. Do you need to call the other resort and ask about it?"

Evan sighed. He dropped down to his ass and propped his arms up on his knees, dangling his hands in front of him. He looked around the resort lobby and sighed again. "Nah, man. It's a lost cause by now, I'm sure. I'll just have to buy another one when I get back home. Or, well, get wherever it is I go from here."

That statement caught Hank's attention, and he said, "So, you met the other Alphas." He left it at that and waited, anticipating Evan's enthusiasm to fill in details. His stomach lurched a little, anxious for his friend.

"Yep," Evan said, and that was all.

Hank's stomach twisted, imagining Evan with Fong, thinking of how Evan had described him, wondering if Evan had been held down by Fong's strong arms.

Or the women—Evan had thought he stood a better chance with the female Alphas. Did they hold him close, kiss his lips, whisper in his ear, and then ride him like there was no tomorrow?

Hank's fists clenched, and his jaw grew tight. He tried to think of something to say to prod Evan into a confession, but before he could Evan jerked his chin up and indicated that Hank should follow the line of his gaze. "That woman seems to want your attention, Hank."

Hank felt his breath quicken when his eyes met Allison's cleavage, and he shifted on his heels as his cock went instantly hard.

Evan's rumbling chuckle next to him penetrated his flare of lust, and he managed to pull his eyes away in time to see Evan make a hubba-hubba face.

"It's not like that," Hank said gruffly. Though it was like that. Just exactly like that.

Hank licked his lips thinking of Allison's apple-flesh and how his teeth might mark it, *had* marked it, had left little scores along the tops of her breasts. He'd tranced before he'd tasted the tips of her apples.

"Sure, Hank. And water isn't wet. Listen, man, I think that's great. You've had luck after all. I'm happy for you." But something about Evan's voice belied his comment.

Speaking of wet, Hank's attention was back on the wet line of sweat collecting delicately between Allison's breasts, and he wanted to know what that tasted like, how it smelled.

Evan shoved his arm a little and said, "What's keeping you here, man? Go over to her. Go on."

He wanted to stand up and go to Allison, but he was scared. The lust was so overwhelming he was afraid he might start licking her chest there in front of everyone. In front of the cameras, which were rolling even now, taking in this conversation with Evan.

"Calm down, Hank," Evan whispered. "You look like you're about to jump out of your skin. Just chill a minute, man, and then go over to her. Take a few deep breaths, clear out your system, and get some control."

Hank felt torn. Something was not quite right; something was definitely wrong. And it wasn't just the cameras taking in every moment and every breath. There was something else.

"Hank, breathe," Evan said, and his hand on Hank's wrist brought Hank back around.

Hank took a deep breath and let it out shakily, and then another.

"Good, that's it."

Hank breathed deeply again, and it was there—Evan's distinct scent, the smell of his warm skin, the tang of his blood running underneath it all. Hank felt a wave of calm descend on him.

"See? A little breathing exercise and all is right with the world. My mother says that if everyone just stopped and really breathed then we'd have world peace."

Hank glanced at Evan who was smiling and seemed to kind of glow from the inside out. "You talk about your mother a lot."

"Do I?" Evan asked, still smiling. "Now, go on. You can do it. No ravishing her at the bar, though, Hank. Take her back to your room for that, man."

Evan pushed at Hank slightly, and with that small shove Hank rose, began to walk toward Allison, only to stop and turn back. "Hey, Evan."

"Yeah?"

"What about you? Did you have good luck?"

Evan shrugged. "Hard to tell, man. Hard to tell. I guess I'll just have to wait and see. Now, go. Shoo. Before she gets bored or thinks you've changed your mind."

Hank nodded and smiled at Evan, turning toward the bar, where he struggled to sit calmly next to Allison for several hours while she talked about God knows what because he couldn't think at all in her presence, but, damn, could he ever *feel*.

✦   ✦   ✦

IT WAS EVENING again and the birds had grown bold in the twilight, screeching in preparation for sleep. Hank stood by the edge of the ocean, trying to ignore the cameras that continued to roll around him. He considered it a success that he'd only broken one camera so far, and only nearly punched one cameraman during the filming. And he wasn't sorry about that. The guy hadn't backed off, and Hank didn't ask twice, not when he was already so over this ridiculous set-up that he could barely see straight. The guy was lucky he hadn't shifted and ripped him open stem to stern.

Allison had gone to her room alone, and he'd been burning with an unsatisfied desire ever since then. He knew she'd been right to leave. It wasn't the time to consummate any kind of bond between them.

Hell, when he was away from her, and down from the high that her scent seemed to provoke in him, he wasn't even sure he liked her.

For one thing, he couldn't hear what she was saying, finding himself so tranced on his lust for her that he couldn't operate beyond faking a laugh when she laughed or nodding mindlessly as her mouth moved. He had no idea what kinds of things he'd agreed to while he was with her; she could have said she thought serial killers had the right idea, and he would have nodded merrily along, clueless to her words.

And that didn't feel safe.

Nothing about the situation felt safe anymore. The cameras, the applicants, the entire scenario made him feel like there wasn't enough room to breathe, like he needed to get out, or to get *in*, or to just be somewhere, anywhere, but here.

Most of all, Hank wanted to get away from the cameras. But he was sick of his suite and sick of the resort's bathrooms—where he hid out far too often. Hell, the guys back at the station in White Edge were going to think he had problems with constipation given how much time he spent in there.

The station—he missed it. He missed the wail of sirens, the way his mountain city felt around him, the smell of it and the rhythm of it, like a heartbeat of its own, pulsing and regular, something he could understand, trace the boundaries of, and protect. There was little to protect here that felt like his own. Just his assigned space, the sycophantic Omegas, and his own body. His own body. God, for some crazy reason, Allison even felt like a threat to the safety of *that*.

It was hard to sleep at night in the resort. The bed was soft and the sheets of the highest quality, but it wasn't home. There were no sounds of *his* city, no evergreen scent wafting in with the pollution through the open windows. He felt anxious when he thought of how he'd left White Edge vulnerable and unprotected to go on this idiotic jaunt in search of an Omega.

Damn David.

Damn the council.

Damn the governor.

Damn all of them.

This entire thing had left the land of Stupid and entered Ludicrous weeks ago.

Hank turned to face the resort and heard the noises from

within—the busy cooks in the kitchen preparing the morning's meal, cutting fruit, and singing songs. The housekeeping staff pushing their rattling trolleys down tiled halls, knocking on rooms, a chorus of cries of "housekeeping" bursting in odd intervals throughout the structure, followed by the white noise of vacuum cleaners, carving hollow spaces in his listening field.

There. It was only when he heard it that he even knew he'd been seeking it.

"The Alpha has strong territorial needs. Any kind of trespass of the boundaries, particularly by another Alpha, can result in a challenge—hostile interaction that can end in violence. Some Alphas have such intense territorial responses that one might say it borders on paranoia—" Evan's voice unspooled across the distance and Hank followed it into the resort and down hallways, passing doorways and passages still listening.

"No, strike that—not paranoia, more like...well, yes, like paranoia."

Hank registered the scribble of pencil on paper and knew Evan was writing—not on a computer, but long hand. It struck him as fitting. He followed the looping scrawling noises after Evan's voice stilled until he found the right door. He glanced behind him at the camera crew that had followed, rolled his eyes, and put his hand in front of the camera.

"Could you just—" he began, and then he groaned and shook his head. "Forget it."

Evan answered at the second knock, distracted and his face covered with streaks of lead, as though he'd absentmindedly scratched at it with the end of his pencil.

"Right, Hank, hi. Come in, just...hold on. I'm in the middle of a thought here." Evan moved out of his way, and Hank shut the door in the face of the camera crew, looking out the peephole to see them debate what to do next and grinning when they finally moved away down the hall.

Evan muttered as he wrote, the words "Alpha" and "territory" coming into play often. It was only after a few minutes that he seemed to remember Hank still stood by the door and he waved toward the bed.

"Sit down. I'll just be a minute. Hold on…yeah, yeah, markers like scent and touch and sound, yeah. Markers. Hmm…" He wrote rapidly, his eyes bright and focused on the paper, his head bent so close that his nose was almost touching it. His body moved in a constant rhythm, as though his excitement at his own thoughts could not be contained.

Hank sat still on the bed watching him, observing how his bare feet jiggled and his ass moved. Evan's heart rate was up enough to cause the front of his shirt to jerk just a little with every beat, and his hair was tangled into a messy ponytail like he'd pulled it back in a hurry. And, yes, closer inspection proved that there was pencil lead there, too. Hank could smell it in the air, academic and somehow cruel, and he could see it in tiny silvery flecks embedded in Evan's curls.

"Hank?"

Hank shook himself. "Ah, yeah. Pencil lead."

"What?"

Hank cleared his throat. "Nothing."

Evan had turned in his seat, his face a little flushed from the creative rush he'd been enjoying, but he was focused on Hank now, and Hank could feel that attention bringing him to center.

Evan said, "So, hi, man. Not that I'm not glad you decided to stop by, but what's the occasion?"

Hank looked around the room. Something was off. "This place has cameras."

Evan nodded. "Yeah, man, all the applicant's rooms are bugged and filmed at all times. Well, until after lights out, thank

God, because I kind of need that alone time, if you know what I mean. Except for the bathrooms; they're never filmed." Evan paused and frowned. "I mean, I guess…I *hope*."

Hank said, "I'm tired of being filmed."

"I bet you are. Hell, I'm tired of it, too. We all are. It'd be nice to just pick your nose, you know, and not worry who might be watching."

Hank stood up and circled the room.

One in the ceiling, completely visible, one nestled behind the mirror, and, yes, he could get that out, and two recording devices in the lamps by the bed, and a final camera attached to the closet door aimed into the bathroom.

Evan watched with wide eyes and an open mouth as Hank systematically pulled each camera and recording device free and destroyed it. The final camera he held up to Evan's face and said, "Any words for the viewing audience?"

"Hi, Mom," Evan said and then smiled when Hank crushed the small camera in his hand. "Whoa-ho, man, intense!"

Hank tossed the broken things in the trashcan and sat down again.

Evan didn't move from his chair but looked at him with amused curiosity flashing over his face.

"So, pick your nose, Captain," Hank said.

Evan laughed, then shoved his middle finger in his nose and wriggled it in and out.

Hank smiled and then laughed, too.

The first deep laugh he'd had in a very long time.

CHAPTER NINE

HE DIDN'T NORMALLY drink much because it did funky things to his senses, but when Evan opened the microfridge in the room and tossed him a beer, Hank popped it open without hesitation and took a long draw.

"Ah, that's good," he breathed.

"Yeah, the real stuff. Mexican beer. Nothing quite like it." Evan took a long gulp and then turned his desk chair around and sat with his arms crossed over the back. "So, what's up? What brings you to Casa del Vaughn?"

Hank shook his head and rolled his eyes, letting out a frustrated breath. "I don't know. I just...I don't know what I'm doing here."

"Doing here in my room, doing here on this show, or doing here on this planet?"

Hank grunted.

"All of it?" Evan surmised.

"Yeah, all of it."

"Okay, man, let's start at the beginning, then. You're here as an Alpha, to protect the humans and shifters, and heck even the little puppies and bunnies of White Edge. That's why you're on this planet." Evan pointed his beer at Hank. "And, believe me, Hank, White Edge needs protection. I mean, hell, just before this show started, back at Spruce, there was that kid who was going to take out an entire classroom during an amphetamine rage. And if it hadn't been for you..."

"That's right. You're at Spruce."

Evan laughed. "Yeah, man, wanna hear a confession?"

"Sure."

"I met you once before at some lame Spruce-sponsored Omega-Alpha mixer. I guess I didn't make much of an impression."

Hank blinked at Evan. "What?" He couldn't imagine meeting Evan and not remembering him. "When was this?"

"I don't know. Sometime last year. It was a really boring party. I didn't go to the next one. Total snooze fest." Evan made snoring noises and rolled his eyes. "I mean, seriously, you'd think that a bunch of Omegas would make for fantastic party people, right? They're intelligent, empathetic, and have been trained to really break through the barriers of the most guarded people in the world, right? Still, they throw the most boring parties I've ever attended. Even here—everyone is so focused on the Alphas that it's hard to have any fun."

"Fun," Hank said, still trying to place Evan in his memory.

"Yeah, you know, Hank, fun. That thing that makes life worth living."

Hank nodded. He couldn't remember the last time he'd had fun, per se. There had been satisfying days, sure, and times when he felt like he could rest at night without too much care, but the last time he'd had fun? Maybe tonight when he'd broken the cameras in Evan's room, with Evan's bright eyes and elevated heartbeat as his audience and applause.

Evan clapped his hands, centering the moment and Hank's attention. "So, Hank, what's up?"

"You know, Captain, I'm sort of tired of all the focus being on me. Let's talk about something else for a change."

"Okay, sure! Like...?" Evan gestured, indicating that Hank should lead.

"I don't know, buddy. I mean you've had all these crazy adventures since we last talked, saw a bunch of Alphas, went to their compounds…so, why don't *you* tell *me* what's up?"

Evan grinned, made another hand gesture that looked like something the rappers on television sometimes did, and said, "Wassup? You wanna know wassup?"

Hank grimaced a little but nodded. "Yeah, sure. Talk to me. About something other than me."

Evan leaned back in his chair and said, "Oh, man, where to start? First, I went to Heather Kallet's resort which was just…weird, man. I don't know. She seemed to like me, kissed me on the cheek at one point, but then it was like…I don't know. She's intense, man. Very intense."

"Intense?"

"Yeah, you know—everything was hard and bright and fast with her. Not much to tell there, man. I don't think she disliked me, but I know I wasn't her number one. I get the impression that no one is her number one. Just herself."

"Selfish," Hank supplied.

"Something like that. Entirely the opposite of Fong, who was incredibly into me, much to my surprise."

Hank's stomach tightened and he pulled on his beer, a long swallow, and then asked as casually as possible, "And how did you feel about him?"

Evan shrugged. "Hard to say. He asked for me on the one-on-one date, and it was pretty romantic, very focused, if you know what I mean."

Hank cleared his throat. "No, sorry, Captain. I don't."

"Well, you know…focused. He was interested. I don't know, though, there might be someone from a prior round. It's impossible to say at this point. I do know, though, that he's a good kisser. A very good kisser." Evan waggled his brows and smiled happily. "Definitely would not have a problem with that aspect of being his Omega."

Hank clenched his jaw and said nothing. He looked down at his beer, gauged that he had half of it left, and decided to pace himself. He didn't like the feelings rushing through him. Somehow he was certain, without a shadow of a doubt, based entirely on a hunch, of course, that Fong was not the right match for Evan. Perhaps the other one, Cameron? Yes, from Atlanta.

"Hank?" Evan asked. "What's wrong?"

"Nothing. Nothing at all. I guess I was just wondering about Cameron."

"Cameron…she's, well, her resort was all about health and fitness. It was more like a spa, actually. I guess if I was going to sum each one up: Heather's place was all business, Fong's place was more pleasure-oriented, you see—couple's massages and champagne all day, fun activities like dolphins and jet skiing and horseback riding—"

"Horseback riding?" Hank asked.

"Yeah, a tour of the island. He took a handful of us."

"He chose you?"

"Yeah," Evan nodded. "Gotta admit it, Hank. You're sort of the most stand-offish of the Alphas participating in this thing."

Hank shrugged. He wasn't sure he cared. He'd never liked investing his time with people he didn't give a damn about; he saw no reason to act any differently here just for the sake of public opinion.

"That doesn't hurt your feelings, does it, man? It's just who you are. You're not here to impress anyone, and I respect that. Entirely. I hear what they're saying, but it's not fun and games. This is our life we're talking about, right? And a lot hangs in the balance here."

"So, you were summing up?" Hank said.

"Right. Well, Cameron is all about health and fitness, meditation, and personal awareness. And you…well, um, heh, big guy, you're all about personal responsibility. I dig it."

"Dig it?"

"Hippie. Mom. Sorry." Evan smiled and then stretched. "So, now that I've spilled, your turn."

Hank could feel the beer swirling through his system, bending things inside of him, and moving other things aside. He felt like he was on the verge of understanding something; he just didn't know what.

"Hank?" Evan said again. "Tell me about Allison. I take it she's the one?"

Hank startled out of his thoughts and focused on Evan again. "Allison? Yeah, maybe."

"Why 'maybe'? She's got your dick on a string, man. Everyone can see that."

Hank scrunched his face, embarrassed that his lust was so obvious and plagued again by doubts about it.

"What? You look like you're in pain."

Hank took a big gulp of the beer, feeling the alcohol in his stomach, waiting as it hit his veins. "Yeah, no. Not pain. It's…I don't think it's a good thing with Allison. That's all."

Evan looked surprised. "Not a good thing? I thought you wanted an Omega. I thought they weren't going to let you keep on being a cop without one." Evan stood up and moved his chair aside, coming to sit next to Hank on the bed. He turned so that one shin pressed against Hank's hip, and he had a full view of Hank's face.

"So, talk to me. What's the problem? She seems great."

"She is great. I…think. I don't know. It's just that when I'm around her—" God, even thinking of her scent made him hard. Hank closed his eyes, embarrassed, and hoped that Evan didn't notice. But, of course he did.

"Ah, I see, man. Too much of a good thing. Makes it so you can't see straight."

"I need an Omega, Vaughn, not a hard-on."

"Right." Evan nodded, deep in thought. "Surely that will go away once you've…you know. Bonded."

Hank snorted. "And if it doesn't? What then? What if I don't even like her once I can…see straight?"

"Come on, Hank, surely you don't think you'd feel this strongly for someone that you wouldn't even like on a personal level."

"Captain, do you think your dick is a good source of counsel?"

Evan looked down at his own crotch speculatively and then sighed. "No, of course not, it's just that this is different, right? I mean, this isn't like anything else you've experienced before, so it has to mean something, don't you think?"

"I don't know."

"But with other women it's been…different, right?"

Hank shrugged. "I don't know. There haven't been a lot of women."

"Come on, Hank. You told me you burned the letters from the old girlfriends, and, look at you, man, there had to have been some women!"

"Not since my Alpha senses came fully online, no. Just my wife." It was a confession that normally would cost him, but, for some reason, talking to Evan, it didn't really hurt to say it. "And with her, I couldn't…not without trancing. Just like that guy you told me about. I…can't."

"Wait…not even with just…you?"

Hank glared at him. Now *that* wasn't something he was going to say aloud.

"Oh," Evan swallowed hard. "Oh, wow. Wow. I had no idea.

I guess I should have had some idea, what with all I've read about Alpha sexuality, but I...well, wow. I see what you mean, man. Yeah."

"Yeah," Hank echoed.

Evan stumbled on, "So, it *was* the sex with your ex-wife, huh? I'm sorry about that, man. I must have come across as so insensitive."

Hank blew out a breath and said, "Don't worry about it, Captain. We all say dumb things sometimes."

Evan nodded, and Hank could tell that he was looking for something funny to say to break the tension, but all that came out was, "Wow."

Hank nodded. It felt strange to finally admit it to someone, but since he'd started really experiencing his Alpha senses full-on, there'd simply never been anyone aside from his wife he was attracted to sexually. Now, whether that was because he was too focused on protecting his territory to really look, or because he'd never met the right woman, he just couldn't say.

But, worse than that, his friendship with his right hand had been over for some time, too. It just never seemed to be enough to get him off, and he was too afraid of trancing all alone with his cock in his hand for God knows how long to really let himself go with it. It'd been quite some time since he'd had an orgasm. Even his dreams had failed to provide him with sexual release. He couldn't trust his judgment now, not when it came to the way Allison made him feel.

"Okay, Hank, I have an idea. This is going to sound crazy, but you're just going to have to trust me." Evan jumped up from the bed and paced in front of him. "Here's the thing, I really think this will help you, and when you think about it, what choice do you have? You either trust me now, or you take a leap of faith with an Omega you're not sure about. What do you want to do here?"

Hank sighed and rubbed a hand over his face. He looked at the microfridge and thought about the bottles of beer inside and took another swig from the one in his fist. He considered asking more questions, but the alcohol pooled in his stomach and dissipated into his system making that seem less important.

Evan nodded, his face serious and calm. "Good. Now, listen, I'll be right back. I'm just going to duck into the bathroom for a second."

Hank continued drinking the beer until it was gone, and then, against his better judgment, he got another one out of the fridge and started on it. He began to feel woozy on the slow, honey-like trip of it, though, and the room tilted a little. Hank realized it wasn't the room, after all, but that he was leaning to the side, sliding down onto the bed.

He glanced at the bottle, only a couple of swallows left in it, and he drank them down, feeling the wonderful release of control, the drunken swoop of the world around him. His eyes went in and out of focus as his ears went wonky bobbing up to the top of the ocean of sound that was the resort, hearing voices from the upper floors. He tried to understand them, but the words were like echoes of actual words. And then he was diving back through layers of sound to the room he was in, and a sudden whimper caught his attention, something close, something important and necessary.

A whimper.

He needed to help someone.

It was only as his eyes slowly opened that he realized he'd closed them at all.

A wolf sat at Evan's desk, gazing at him with blue eyes, one paw raised, and the small whimpers were issuing from his throat. Something welled inside Hank, a sound, a noise, a response—a roar, and he blinked, holding it in, resisting the urge to shift.

Yes, he'd blinked, and yet the wolf stayed, watching him, whimpering. Hank turned toward the bathroom and called out, "It looks like you've got a wolf in your room, Captain."

And then he started to laugh, but it wasn't really very funny. He hiccupped and threw the empty bottles on the floor, lying down on the bed, staring at the wolf across from him.

"So, pal, what's going on?"

The wolf cocked its head, put its paw down, and whined.

"Well, aren't you going to say anything?" Hank tried to remember if the wolf ever talked in his dreams. He didn't think so. "Your bear friend isn't here," Hank said, feeling the lie of it. He was the bear after all. He wanted to shift and become the bear for this beautiful, trusting wolf.

The wolf whimpered again and Hank sat up on the bed. "Are you hurt, buddy?"

"Who are you talking to, Hank?" Evan's voice was loud in the quiet room, and Hank realized he'd been listening so hard for the wolf to speak that he'd focused his senses.

Hank jerked his eyes toward Evan in the doorway, hair up and still smelling of cruel pencil lead, but also of soap and water.

"Hank?"

Hank shook his head, trying to think clearly. "The wolf…" he said, trailing off, knowing that when he looked back the animal would be gone. Now that Evan was in the room with him, there was nothing there.

"Wolf?" Evan asked.

"Forget it. This was a bad idea." Hank said, sitting up further and trying to figure out if he could get back to his room without tipping over, and if he should even try.

"Wow, man, you're tanked," Evan said. His voice was close now, his breath hot by Hank's ear as Evan's arms propped him up, scooted him back on the bed toward the headboard and the pillows. "On just one beer? Really?"

"'S'right." Hank said, pointing at him. "I told you. You said you knew." Hank wanted to say more but his tongue felt so thick that he wasn't sure that he could.

"Well, yeah, I knew, but I didn't *know*." Evan seemed to be considering him seriously, and Hank turned and looked him in the eye, staring at him as Evan evaluated *something*.

"Bad idea," Hank said again.

"Wait," Evan said, his voice a little shaky. "I don't know. I mean, it might be a bad idea, but I think we should try it anyway."

Hank shook his head, slumped down on the pillows, and said, "Nah. I should go to sleep now. I'm going to have enough of a hangover tomorrow."

Evan crawled up next to him on the bed. He was shaking. Hank could feel it vibrating through the bed.

"What's got you so keyed up, Captain?" Hank yawned and the world seemed to enter through his mouth. He could taste the sea, the clouds, and the stars. He let it all out and shook his head again, trying to get free of the sensory overload. "I'll be okay tomorrow. Soon as it wears off. Shouldn't have listened to you, though."

Evan's nervous swallow was as loud as a thunderclap. "Shh, Hank. Let me just try, okay? For you."

"Try what? I think you've tried enough." He didn't know what he meant by that, but it had something to do with the fresh spunk scent lingering on Evan's freshly washed hands, the whimpering of the wolf, and the description of Fong's kisses.

"No, listen to me." Evan scooted beside him, rested along the length of him in a way that was pretty intimate, and Hank scooted instinctively away, but Evan followed close behind.

"Think about Allison, okay, man? What is it that you like best about her? Is it her hair, her smile? What really gets you going?"

Hank gritted his teeth together as a wave of lust rushed over him. Autumn apple scent and a warm heartbeat under soft skin. Oh, God, he was so hard it hurt.

"Yeah, okay, think about that some more. She's warm, and she smells good, like…what?"

"Apples," Hank muttered. Crisp fall mornings surrounded by fallen apples, the bubble-gum pink of Silvia's sweater, the flash of her silver braces, and her blonde hair in the breeze. "Autumn. Harvest."

"Yeah, she's warm, and crisp, and somehow wholesome. I see that, Hank. I see that."

Hank was twitching with want and need, his cock aching and jerking in his pants, wanting touch so badly. Evan's breath was hot and damp and close to his ear as he whispered, "Hank, I've got my eyes closed, you can touch yourself if you need to, man, I won't look. I'm just here to keep you from trancing, okay? If you want to…go ahead."

Hank shook his head. No way in hell was he putting on a show for Evan. He swallowed hard and tried to force himself to move, to leave, but his cock was aching, and Evan was talking again, saying something important, but Hank decided he wouldn't listen, and yet he did. It was crazy.

"She's just two stories above us, Hank. Can you smell her? Try. Focus and smell her, think about it, find her scent."

Hank was shaking now, but he found himself obeying Evan's voice, his nose sifting through musty wood floorboards, the dusty carpets, the musky scent of body odor, and the foul scents of bathrooms, and then he found it: the smell of warm rushing blood wrapped in memories of his first crush.

Silvia, fifteen years old, and older than him by several years.

Apples had surrounded them, sun-warm and plump, juicy. Silvia fed him one once, juice from it running down the palm of her hand, onto her wrist, and he'd leaned forward, licked it, tasted the sweetness of her skin, and then she'd shoved him. There had been air, and a breathless drop to the earth. He'd smacked his back on a branch on the way down, and Silvia's voice, half-scared, half-angry, calling down to him, and even then she'd looked full of sweetness, backed by the sunlight in the sky.

Hank had lain on the ground staring up at her, and she'd been an angel to him. Apples had never tasted so sweet.

"Silvia," Hank whispered, understanding flooding him.

"Yeah?" Evan asked, his voice confused but warm.

"Oh, God," and Hank arched up off the bed, his cock twitching and shooting, breaking into orgasmic release as the memories filled him up.

Silvia in the sunlight, and little Hank in his bed, hand under the covers moving so fast, and, God, the world had exploded in pleasure for the first time, wet, spurting, convulsing pleasure, and afterward Hank could still taste the apples and her skin.

"Silvia," he said again, jerking on the bed, coming, and he leaned into Evan's hand on his arm, voice in his ear.

"Relax, yeah, there. Just there. Good. Hank, you're doing so good. It's okay, stay here, don't go too far. Just…right here."

Hank shook and shivered, the orgasm lasting far longer than he remembered possible. He quivered and ached, falling back to the earth, the scent of apples replaced by Evan's warm skin and the sharp cut of pencil lead, and he opened his eyes.

Evan leaned over him, his blue eyes big and worried, the light behind him obscuring his expression, but his concern evident in his voice. "Okay, Hank? Are you okay?"

Hank blinked and stared at him, trying to get control of his emotions that ricocheted between ecstasy and joy, mortification and anger, and even gratitude. He growled, feeling the protective bear rising. Fur sprouted from his skin and he moaned at the familiar crushing pain of his organs realigning, his bones breaking and shifting.

Evan swallowed hard and nodded his head. "It's okay, Hank. It's good. *You're* good."

Hank stood and roared. Pleasure still raged in him, contained only by his bear form rising to the surface. Vulnerable and exposed, it was his only protection.

"Take a deep breath. You don't want to shift right now, man. It's okay."

But Hank did want to shift. He knew he could ground himself in Evan, that he'd be safe again there, but he also knew he didn't want to have to remember the part of his life that came after that first understanding of lust and the loss that had nearly destroyed him.

"Go," Hank boomed, his body cracking and growing, the bear taking over him. "Get out! Go!" The last word became a roar.

Evan's eyes flew wide. "I'll, uh, yeah. But I could help you? Okay, okay, no, I'll go. I'll, um, leave you alone now. Okay? Yeah. But if you need me, I'll be...well, you can find me if you..."

Evan backed away from him carefully. He flung his thumb toward the door and said, "I'll just..."

Then he turned and left, opened the door. As claws burst through his fingertips, Hank heard Evan's call out to the camera crews. "He's shifting. Don't come any closer and don't make any sudden sounds or moves. If you don't hear any screaming, then I've got it under control. Understand?"

Then Evan came back into the room, the door closed behind him. He held out his hands in a placating gesture, and his blue eyes gazed at him pleadingly. "I know you told me to go, but I want to be here for you. I care about you, Hank. I don't want you to do anything you'd regret. Take some slow breaths and come back to me now, okay? Stay here with me, in your human skin. All right, man? Get me?"

Hank gazed at him and then sat back down on the bed. He was half-shifted, but when Evan sat down beside him, placing one hand on Hank's knee and the other on his back, and began to sing a lullabye, the reversal of his transformation began.

Bones cracked back. His claws retracted. Hank dropped back on the bed, his head back to the pillows and listened hard to Evan's voice. He stared at the ceiling above, seeing the molecules, the particles, the mesmerizing nature of it. And he didn't trance.

The fur sank back into his skin, and he was himself again. He breathed in and out slowly, drifting in a weird place, trying to figure out how he felt.

Evan kept singing.

And Hank kept coming back to one thing, seeking the beautiful, quick heartbeat of the man who'd brought him here. As Evan slowed his singing, Hank reached out and took hold of his hand. Quietly, under his breath, he whispered, "Captain…"

They curled into each other and said nothing more until sleep claimed them both.

CHAPTER TEN

About midnight Hank crawled out of the window of Evan's room, leaving him sleeping on the bed, a tangle of hair and blankets and still in his jeans and T-shirt. Hank managed to scale down the side of the building using balconies as footholds, stumbled over some roots from the shrubbery, and twisted his ankle. He limped down to the sea. He knew the moment the camera crews spotted him. They started shooting and closing in all around. He stood motionless staring out at the ocean, tossing darkly in the night. He missed his home. He missed the forest. He missed the mountains.

A hand on his arm got his attention.

"Hank?" It was Warren. The guy with the microphone. The host of the show. "Hank, did something happen with you and Evan earlier tonight?"

Hank's lips twisted, and he snorted. He shook from free from Warren and said, "If you don't get that thing out of my face and you don't get these assholes to leave me alone, someone's going to get hurt."

Warren's face blanched even in the darkness. Hank was momentarily grateful for whatever it was that gave Alphas that terrifying edge that pushed others away. Warren nodded and backed off, and though Hank had a hard time believing it, the camera crews disappeared too.

He sank down into the sand, feeling the soft give of it under his ass, and he let himself think, really think, about something he'd never considered. A male Omega. It terrified him.

The glisten of the moon on the waves brought to mind Silvia's braces, the way they'd shimmered in the sunshine. Amazingly, thoughts of Silvia no longer hurt him the way they had for years. He felt relaxed, deeply contented, and like a hard, hurtful part of him had finally given way inside. Silvia had been his coach's daughter. Coach Terrell, who'd taught his football team, had always encouraged him, telling him to follow his gut, unaware of how much the simple words "trust yourself" had meant to him. Especially coming from a family who encouraged him to suppress his shifter abilities out of bias and fear.

And Silvia had also been Justin's sister. Justin, who'd been Coach's effeminate disappointment and Hank's friend, maybe even his best friend. Hank had never been able to tell Justin the truth about himself, had never told him about being an Alpha, or how Justin's steady hand on his wrist when they were trekking through the woods had kept Hank focused and even led him out of early trances.

Hank sighed and shook his head. It was obvious now that he was allowing himself to think about these things: Justin had been his first Omega, even if they'd been too young to truly bond. Even if they didn't even know what that meant back then.

It would have been a hard time for any kid, but when his powerful Alpha senses first began to burble to the surface at the same time as adolescence began to change his body, his father had been first unavailable, then disbelieving, and finally cruel. Home had never been a safe place, and when it was evident that Hank couldn't avoid outing himself as a shifter, it became unbearable.

And then Justin had died. A homophobic jock from their school had beaten him to death. Hank had found his body. And nothing was ever the same again. Hank had shifted fully for the first time, hunted down the boy who'd done it, and dealt out justice in his own way. It was the fear of all humans—an alpha who didn't wait for the wheels of justice to do their crushing work. And so, abandoned by his family and in trouble with the council, he'd been sent to live in the mountains with the White Moon tribe to learn how to deal with his grief and control his anger.

But after Justin's death, Hank swallowed his Alpha senses, shoved them down, tucking them inside so deeply that he started to shift uncontrollably. The Alpha of White Moon, Krushreet, became his mentor and taught him, little by little, to open up to his Alpha-ness again. He helped Hank embrace his duty, even if he never fully let go of the idea that Justin's death had been his fault. If he'd admitted the depth of his emotions for his friend, cared for him better, protected him more, then the homophobic prick would never have gotten a chance to hurt Justin.

Once he'd healed enough to be in control of himself, he noticed there were several Omegas he'd learned to depend on within the White Moon tribe, but he remained unbonded, because he was waiting. Waiting for what?

Waiting for the woman who glistened in the sun and smelled of apples like Silvia? Or waiting for the boy like Justin? The one who accepted him completely and didn't even blink twice when he tranced? The one who touched him with such tenderness and confidence?

A sudden shudder went through him hard as the memory of finding Justin's dead body rocked him. God, was that it? Was it Justin's body destroyed and empty that had kept him from ever thinking about a male Omega? Even now?

Hank's eyes clouded over and he pressed his forehead to his knees, allowing himself to drift for just a moment on memories of Silvia's smile, Justin's face, and Coach's encouraging voice. The smell of his tears as they mixed with the sand was confirmation.

Hank didn't want to lose, didn't want to feel that abandoned and hurt ever again. Never again.

The fall from the apple tree had been ecstasy, but the fall into hell when he found Justin's body had been endless, and maybe it was still going on. Maybe he still hadn't hit bottom.

Daylight was coming. He could smell it on the air. He lifted his head and realized he'd spent the night lost in memories, lost in thought. When he stood up, he could feel them behind him, the production crew, the potential Omegas, the resort staff, the doctor with his medicines, all of them standing there waiting to see what was happening, unsure of what to do.

Hank took a deep breath, and, yes, Evan was there, too.

Turning around, he saw Evan standing in front of the crowd, his arms out to his sides, as though holding everyone else back, and his honest eyes were scared, nervous, and wide.

Hank nodded at him tersely, and Evan dropped his arms. They all came at him then like ants or soldiers or solid bits of matter drawn inexorably toward a larger object, a tide, a gravitational pull.

All except for Evan who stood by the steps to the resort, his hands in his pockets, his hair blowing in the wind, and an expression on his face that told Hank that he was on his own with this one. Evan had done all that he intended to do, and Hank's stomach lurched as Evan turned and walked away.

"Hank, are you okay?" Allison's voice in his ear was fine, quite lovely really, but nothing special.

He nodded at her words and began to ward off the others, shaking free from the doctors, saying, "It's fine. Leave it. Get back. Just...*back off.*"

Hank heard Warren rattling on to the camera that eccentricities such as staring at the ocean all night were common with Alphas, and that while they had not seen such strange acts from the other three participating in the program, it could be explained by the fact that Alpha Morrow had only accepted his Alpha abilities later in life, which could lead to a higher level of difficulty adjusting them to fit in with social niceties.

"As you might imagine," Warren continued. "Whatever Omega such an Alpha as Morrow chooses for his own will need to be prepared to accept these behaviors and to deal with an Alpha who is perhaps a bit of a misanthrope."

✦　✦　✦

DAVID SAT ALONE on his sofa with a cup of soup and his remote by his side. He blinked at the television screen, adjusted his glasses, and blinked some more. Nothing changed. Morrow was still obviously falling into a bond with Evan, and yet seemed unable to cope with that fact.

Or to even acknowledge it.

David sighed. He was glad he was alone. If he were at the station with the other idiots, he'd probably have to be slapping some heads right about now. Instead, he could sit and fret over his best detective and the city's Alpha alone.

He'd wondered how it was all going to play out.

Evan had definitely thrown himself very willingly into the running with all three other Alphas, and the date with Fong had been pretty steamy. It'd left David nearly frothing at the mouth on Hank's behalf, frankly, even though Hank, the idiot, hadn't made any kind of claim at all at that point.

Still, something had happened the prior night in Evan's room. Anyone could see that. But the kid wasn't talking, and Hank was freaking out. It was a mess. This entire thing was a mess.

David felt a wave of horror and embarrassment for Hank that

his most intimate feelings were being broadcast loud and clear for the world to see and speculate about.

The day before, David had seen Hank's face on a tabloid in the supermarket, and a quick perusal had disturbed him mightily. Questions about whether internalized homophobia could be overcome in an Alpha/Omega situation had plagued the article. And a psychiatrist, who 'did not know or treat either Vaughn or Morrow,' spoke about supposed evidence that Hank was a bigot, implying that was why he couldn't recognize his attraction to Evan.

David had gotten so pissed off that he'd thrown the magazine on the floor of the supermarket. Morrow wasn't a homophobe; he was just the least self-aware man on the damn planet. That was all. But stuff like that didn't sell magazines, and the tabloid press was *not* going to give the man a break. That much was evident.

As he cleaned up his dinner, rinsing out the cup of soup and washing the spoon, David thought about what he'd learned about Evan. The kid seemed to be pretty brilliant. He'd be a real asset to their team in the PD, and David thought he'd even be able to get past all that annoying and boundless energy if the kid could contribute not only to a better Hank, but provide his own observations on cases as well.

David went to bed early, his mind preoccupied, and he dreamed of sending a secret message to Hank. When he woke the next day, he shook his head and chuckled, asking, "And what the hell did that mean?"

The message had been, "Choose the wolf."

CHAPTER ELEVEN

PPARENTLY THE PSYCHIATRISTS told the camera crews to back off from Morrow. It was the final day of this little social experiment anyway, and the time had come. Hank would meet with the other three Alphas that night in a tribal circle inside of a television set built for the purpose, and each would make their claim on an Omega, or, as Hank intended, no one at all.

The other applicants avoided him, too, including Allison, and, more importantly, Evan. Hank wandered the length of the coastline marking his territory over and over, kicking at the sand, watching the birds, and thinking in rhythmic circles like the waves. A rush of memory in, a tide of thought out, then another wave of emotion to deal with, sometimes strong and smothering, other times smooth and sweet.

Hank toed the line where the wet sand met the dry and waited.

It was late afternoon, only hours before the tribal fire that would put an end to this mockery, when Evan showed. He stood at the bottom of the stairs leading down from the resort for a long time, his hands in his pockets, his hair in the wind, and his face carefully neutral. Hank fought the urge to call for him, to wave him over, knowing that it had to be on Evan's terms, that he had to see if Evan had the balls to come to him after Hank had shifted in front of him and then slept in his arms.

The first step was full of hesitation, but then he walked with a certain stride, his eyes on the horizon instead of Hank and his back ramrod straight. His face, though, reflected all his uncertainty, and he stood quietly by Hank for a long time before he said, "I'm clean, man. No recording devices. Nothing. We can talk."

Hank nodded, his eyes scanning the line of the land and then the sea again.

"We *need* to talk," Evan said again.

"Yeah, about that," Hank said. "Maybe some more talking should have happened last night before we tried your little experiment."

Evan nodded, his eyes unguarded as always.

"A little consent goes a long way."

"Hank, look, I couldn't know what would happen…"

"Cut the crap, Evan. You knew. Or suspected. Isn't that what you thought *should* happen?"

Evan took the verbal hits like a pro, accepting the accusation and offering no defense. "You're right, Hank. I wanted it to happen. I kind of hoped it would. I admit, I sort of thought it would be good for you."

"You're not my Omega, Evan."

"I overstepped," Evan murmured.

"Overleaped," Hank corrected.

Evan's swallow was wet and thick, and Hank wanted to touch his throat, feel it squeeze the saliva down, but he forced his hands to remain still.

"Do you want honesty?" Evan asked.

Hank said, "Probably for the best at this point."

"You have to believe me, Hank, I never thought that last night would happen. I didn't plan it, or contemplate it, or really think it through at the time. I know I should be sorry, Hank, for pushing you so far and so fast, and, in a big way, I am. Sorry that you feel hurt, that you're uncomfortable. Sorry that you were vulnerable and that you regret that. Sorry that what we did made you shift. But, the truth is that, in a really big way, I don't regret it, either, because seeing you that way, so open and letting me in? Seeing you shift? God, it was the biggest high of my life, man. The most exciting thing I could have imagined. Like scaling Everest or something. The ultimate for me."

"Too bad I was intoxicated when you proposed the idea."

Evan's guilt marred his face but then he stared into Hank's eyes with an unexpected challenge. "I didn't make you drink those beers, Hank. And can you honestly say you'd have gone there with me or with *anybody* sober? With Allison? Can you?"

Hank clenched his jaw, pulled his eyes away, and watched the ocean churn. "Honestly, Captain?"

Evan lifted his brows expectantly.

"No. But it still didn't give you the right to take me there when I wasn't sober, either."

Evan's face hurt Hank to look at, the guilt and the devastation, even more the disappointment. Hank could smell Evan's roiling stomach, the sick feeling under his fear.

Evan kicked the sand and said, "In White Edge, when I saw you at the mixer, I watched you all night long. I had you nailed, completely pegged as the ultimate loner Alpha. The kind of guy who ends up dying because he can't bond." Evan shook his head and squinted at the setting sun. "Truth is, Hank, when I saw you on the list for this, I couldn't believe it. Hank Morrow? The man I'd met was so shut off, so disinterested… And, let me make this clear, because I want you to be absolutely sure of this—I never thought even for a minute that I stood a chance with you. But it was your name that made me sign up. For some reason, I thought, if Morrow takes this path, then you should look into it, too. So, I did."

Hank grunted, not sure what purpose this confession served.

"I may have come here because of you, Hank," Evan went on. "But I didn't come here *for* you. Let's be clear on that, okay? Do you understand what I'm saying here, man?"

"Not really, Evan. No."

"I'm saying that now, having met the other Alphas, and after…well, after last night in my room…." Evan cleared his throat, turned and met Hank's gaze with an open expression, like the wolf in Hank's dream laying on his back, his stomach there for the bear to rip open with his claws. "I'm telling you now that I'd like to be your Omega. I think I'd be good at it, and I think you need me."

Hank scoffed, but Evan grabbed his arm. "Just hear me out, okay? I've thought about it. I get along great with Fong. He's funny, and he's smart, and he seemed to really like my body, which is great, you know, fantastic."

Hank jerked his arm away, stuffing down the urge to grab Evan and inspect him for evidence of this Fong's manhandling, disturbed at the strength of that desire.

"And Heather, damn, man, she's beautiful. Stunning really, though I get the vibe that she's playing me, and that makes me uncomfortable in deep and scary ways." Evan shook himself. "But I might be wrong. It's just that something about her makes me think of you and want to be near you so I can feel safe, and that tells me all I need to know about Heather."

Hank felt his panic rising, his hands itching to grab Evan and look him over from top to bottom, to sniff him and make sure he still smelled the right way. God, how had it never occurred to him that Evan would be an option for the other Alphas? Of course he'd known that, he'd wished him luck, and he hadn't been insincere at the time. But he hadn't *known*.

Evan went on, "And Cameron? She's fine. Boring really. Very into yoga and meditation, which you would think would be right up my alley, but somehow makes me think of my mother, and that's no good, man. No good at all."

Evan shook his head, his lips twisted in amused disturbance at his thoughts, but then he was back, looking right into Hank's eyes and saying, "But it's more than that. It's not even like the others aren't good enough for me so you're the best leftover choice or something. Because, I'm sure it isn't news to you that you're taciturn and cranky and generally detached and hard to know. Man, your issues are *legion*, and God help whoever has to help you sort through those, do you know what I mean?"

Evan chuckled a little, but his smile faded when he saw that Hank was *not* smiling back. "But I like that, I guess. Or something. I like it a lot. Just, when I'm with you, Hank, I feel…well, it's like something kind of clicks. Don't tell me you haven't noticed it. It was there right from the start. Like old friends or like…"

"Soul mates?" Hank said, snorting in disgust.

"Hey man, you said it," Evan said, pushing his hair out of his face to see Hank better. "So make of that what you will."

"Right," Hank replied. "Now, get out of here. We both have some place we need to go."

Evan pressed his lips together and nodded, turning to walk away.

Hank fixed his eyes away from the retreating back, but he could hear Evan go—the fast rhythm of his heart, the spasm of him clearing his throat, and Hank smelled the scent of tears, unfallen, but there all the same, mixed in with the usual scent of Evan's skin.

Hank noted the absence of pencil lead this morning, and his heart clenched at the flash of memory—Evan at his desk, his bare feet jiggling, his mouth moving as he scribbled down words.

Hank kicked the sand hard. Kicked it and sat down. He was

screwed and he didn't care if he was late.

✦   ✦   ✦

AFTER HE'D SHOWERED and put on the khaki pants and button-up shirt he'd chosen for the tribal fire, Hank stared at himself in the mirror. His mind skirted over a memory of Justin, dangling upside down from the apple tree that Silvia had pushed Hank from after he licked her.

Justin's smile had been bright like stars in the desert, and they'd done things together—things that boys sometimes do in the heat of the moment. Hank remembered a hot hand on his cock, not his own, the rush and whisper of Justin's voice, and the sudden sting of a slap on his face. That'd been the beginning of the end—that moment with Justin and the sleeping bags zipped together, and Hank's father's hand across his face.

Then Justin had been murdered, and Hank had avenged him. But no one else seemed to think that was a good thing. Not even Coach, who had grown silent and angry, his back turned to Hank. He never said a kind word to him again, as though it was Hank's fault that his son had died. Silvia's sweet smile never made it out of braces, soured by her loss. Even now when he ran into her at the White Edge market or in the mall, hauling four children around in a minivan, she never smiled for him, only sighed and said, "Do you still remember my brother, Hank?"

And he did.

Hank had remembered even as he'd tried to block out the way the sun had played in Justin's hair, and how Hank's heart and cock had stirred looking at him, just like when he'd looked at Silvia, only it was different between them, because he knew Justin felt the same.

He'd blocked out the way Justin's face collapsed with orgasm, and the smell of his cum, and the times they'd held each other after, whispering that they'd never tell a soul what they'd done. But they had to try that again soon. When? Now.

Justin, swinging from the apple tree.

Justin, laughing in the breeze by the river, a fish on his line, and his eyes shining just for Hank.

Justin, and then Silvia, and then Coach—all of them stood in front of him in his mind's eye, gazing at him somberly, and finally Krushreet, covered in his paint, appeared, too, to whisper in his ear, "Haven't you punished yourself enough, Hank?"

The steam from the shower had long since dissipated, and the bathroom was left chilly and covered with small drops of cold water. Hank heard the producers edging toward his room warily, whispering in tight voices about whether or not they dared to knock on his door.

Hank gazed into his own eyes, thinking of wolves baring their stomachs, fear running through him like ice-cold rapids. Was he safe? Was he lovable? Was this truth something he could deal with? Was he punished enough?

"I don't know, Krushreet," Hank whispered. "I don't know."

CHAPTER TWELVE

HANK WAITED IN his area, agitated and pacing the floor. He could *feel* the other Alphas nearby, hear their pulses, and smell them. He knew they paced their small rooms as well, awaiting the moment when they would all meet. As the viewing audience had been warned, it was possible sparks could fly.

Hank heard Warren speaking rapidly into his microphone about the exciting evening ahead. "Each Alpha has chosen two, that's right *two*, final candidates for selection as an Omega. But what makes this extra exciting tonight is, as you may have noticed, two of the five final candidates have been chosen as finalists by two Alphas. Ladies and gentlemen, we aren't entirely sure what might happen here. This could lead to a challenge."

Hank's stomach churned and he clenched and unclenched his fists, fighting the urge to snarl. He wasn't taking on an Omega. He'd already decided that, so he didn't understand why the word challenge raised his hackles so thoroughly. It was almost like he wanted it. Ached for it even.

Flesh ripping under his hands and tearing between his teeth. He itched for it.

Wallace kept taping, "Assuming their proposal is accepted by their selected Omega, the bonding ceremony will take place in one of these amazing rooms at the respective resort of each Alpha. Yes, that's right, ladies and gentlemen, as you'll recall, bonding is a primarily supernatural experience, unexplainable but necessary for the full functioning of the Alpha and Omega partnership.

"Bonding takes place during the titillating activity we all refer to as S. E. X." Warren whispered as he spelled, and said, "This is a family show, of course, so we won't be viewing *that* portion of the evening. I know, I know, I hear the disappointed groans through the screen, but let us assure you the Alphas will need their privacy for *that*."

Hank rolled his eyes and paced the room even more frantically. It was ridiculous. He didn't understand the fascination with Alphas and Omegas. But, to take it to this level? To reduce the Alpha and Omega bonding experience to the equivalent of a naked wedding night caper was an insult. Making it some kind of romantic story for children to hear and begin to dream of was reductionist. It's not enough to want to be a princess these days; no, much better to be an Omega or an Alpha. Yes, kiddos, televise your desperation and have the moment that changes it all talked about like it's nothing more than a celebrity's latest sex story in the *National Enquirer*. It really chapped his ass to think about it.

And, damn, if the scent of the other Alphas wasn't making him crazy. He felt like climbing the walls. He had to take deep breaths to keep from breaking the door open and setting out on his own. His hands were in fists, and his breath came in heavy pants when the door opened and one of the producers stepped in. His face was pale and sweaty, and he stood as close to the door as possible.

"Yeah?" Hank asked, pacing back and forth, unable to hold still.

"Mr. Morrow." The guy wiped his face with a handkerchief and smiled, reeking of fear. "There's been a change of plans. It seems that we can't possibly put you all in the same room. As it is, you're all nearly breaking down the walls. It was foolish of us to assume…to think it possible…"

A loud crash and roar had Hank crouching low and ready. The producer said quickly, "We're moving you back to your resorts. We'll tape from there. Prepare yourself."

Hank shook his head, grabbed the producer, and said, "No. We finish this. Now."

The producer quaked in his hands, and Hank had to force himself to release him. "You've set us on all edge, bated us with Omegas, and played mind games with us for weeks. Finish it. Or I finish you."

Hank actually felt he might make good on the threat, his heart racing and his throat tight. He needed it to be over, and he could feel it, pulsing through the air around him, the other Alphas needed it to be over, too.

"It's not safe," the producer whispered.

"Surprise, surprise," Hank countered, shoving him aside and leaving the room he'd been holed up in for far too long. "Sometimes you get exactly what you asked for."

It seemed he wasn't alone in his impatience. Fong was the first one he met. The man moved elegantly, dangerously, and they paced the floor around each other for a moment before they were joined by Heather, a blonde snarling bit of womanhood, who proved she could hold her own when Fong made a move toward her, and she kicked him halfway across the room. Hank snorted his appreciation and crouched down, ready to fight, too.

Cameron's voice was calm, collected, as she stood to the side. "Stop it," she said. "Now. We are in neutral territory. This is no one's ground. Chill out. All of you."

Hank eyed Heather, who glanced between Fong and Hank, and they all dropped their stances simultaneously.

"Christ, let's get this over with," Heather said, tossing her hair. Her eyes were tense and wild. "I'm about to lose my mind."

"Welcome to the jungle," Fong said, glancing between them.

Heather narrowed her eyes. "Lay off the puns, asshole."

Fong smirked and tossed his black hair out of his eyes. "And you should stay away from the bottle blonde, darling."

Heather's lip curled threateningly, but Cameron spoke up again. "Do any of you want to collect an Omega tonight? Yes? Good. Focus, please. For God's sake."

Hank said, "She's right. Let's stay focused and get the hell away from each other as soon as possible. Let's just get this thing over with."

"You said it," Heather said, sniffing the air. "This way."

They could all smell them.

The little group of Omegas that were left, culled from the herd of obsequious Omegas that had passed in front of them over the prior weeks. Hank could smell the stink of their sweat, the anxious kind that was more putrid than any other, and he could smell the detergent in their clothes, the smoke from a quick cigarette. He could smell sage, sandalwood, and shampoo, and if he opened his mouth and gulped the air, tasting it and smelling it both, he could detect that cruel pencil lead scent, though just barely.

They were waiting for them. Waiting to be chosen.

The fire was high and burning steadily. The group stood beside it, none of them talking, all of them nervous, and their expressions were of shock and surprise to see all four Alphas entering together.

"I…thought we were…moving…or something," Allison whispered to Evan.

Evan, staring at Hank, shook his head and swallowed, saying nothing.

"If you want this on tape," Heather said to the cameramen, "better start rolling."

They scrambled to hoist their cameras and boom microphones, desperate to catch it all. As the producers and Warren ran into the room, Fong stepped forward, his dark eyes bright and his smile predatory.

"I go first," he announced and there was a tense moment when Hank thought there would be a challenge to that, but Heather looked to Cameron, gritted her teeth, and rolled her eyes, giving her consent.

Hank's stomach tightened as he watched Fong's eyes linger on Evan, looking him over from head to toe in a way that made Hank want to punch him. Evan was brilliant, an anthropologist, and he deserved better than some pleasure-motivated Alpha who would force him to submit to sensual hot stone massages and drawn-out sex with oils and food and God knows what else. Hank's jaw clenched and he started shaking. What the hell was he thinking about? Evan would probably love that.

"I choose Joe," Fong said, stepping forward to grab the arm of the guy that Hank remembered as the one with the cowboy hat who hadn't annoyed him. "Any challenge?" Fong called over his shoulder as he wrapped his arms around his selection.

Hank kept his eyes on Evan, watching for a reaction, strangely wanting to punch Fong for *not* choosing Evan almost as much as he'd wanted to punch him when he thought he was going to choose him. Who wouldn't choose Evan? He was the entire package. The full deal. Hank's fists unclenched a little, though, when he saw a wave of relief sweep over Evan's face, and he smelled the release of tension as Evan exhaled.

Fong and Joe immediately started kissing in a way that was so lewd and intense that Hank was quite sure it wasn't appropriate for a family show. The room suddenly wafted with their pheromones, and Hank and the other Alphas reacted immediately, shifting from foot to foot, fur popping out and retreating again. Everyone was edgy, and the atmosphere in the room ratcheted up another notch.

No one spoke, and all eyes turned to Hank. "Go on then," Heather said. "Take your pick."

Hank shook his head. "Women first."

Heather snarled, "I don't need your condescension."

"Just trying to be polite," Hank gritted out, his urge to fight for territory, any territory, incredibly strong with so many Alphas stalking around the same small enclosure.

Cameron stepped forward then and said, "Listen, I already know who I want. Hank, take your pick. Now. Even my patience is growing thin."

Hank cleared his throat and looked directly at Evan. "I choose no one. I didn't find an Omega."

There was a shudder through the room then. He saw out of the corner of his eye that Heather was looking at him in disgust, and Cameron with an expression of pity. Evan's face was serious and lined, and if it hadn't been for the change in his breathing, a tightness, Hank might have believed that what he'd said hadn't hurt.

Hank felt immediately sick, as though someone had punched him in the gut, and he took in gulping breaths, trying to stem the aggression that seemed ready to overwhelm him. He felt wild and torn between pushing Evan out of the room so that he wouldn't have to see him there, breathing in and out in that wounded way, and pulling Evan to him and giving in to his damned inherent bisexuality right there in that room with all the world watching. And then another part of him just wanted to beat the hell out of every Alpha there until none of them were left standing.

Cameron looked to Heather, who chose some guy named Rich that Hank didn't remember meeting. Blond, brown eyes, and kind of gullible looking. Easy prey. So easy that Hank could imagine snapping his neck.

The thought made him blink, shocked at himself. Things were getting out of hand, his emotions flying out of control, and he needed to rein them in before things got…dangerous. He chuckled then. Things had been dangerous from the moment this whole thing started.

Cameron took a deep breath and spoke. "Evan? Would you consider being my Omega?"

Hank's stomach lurched and he stared at Evan, who didn't look at him. His chest felt tight and he couldn't breathe right, the room was too small, way too small, and he was moving, because he couldn't not, and yes, there were way too many Alphas in his territory, moving toward his territory, getting ready to touch—

"Challenge," Hank yelled, not knowing where the word came from, not having planned to say it, not even knowing for sure why, but if Cameron touched Evan, if she moved another muscle toward him, there would be no more time for warning; Hank was sure of that.

"Oh, come on, Hank," Cameron said, putting her hands on her hips and looking at him in disbelief. "You had your chance. You passed. For fuck's sake, asshole, make up your mind."

Hank's lips were tight, his jaw flexed, and his eyes focused on Cameron's pissed off face. "Challenge," he repeated. "Where do you want to fight?"

"Now. Here."

"Wait, wait, wait," Evan's voice wavered in the room. "Fight? *What?* Let's just calm down and talk this out."

Hank saw that Evan had stepped into his line of attack. He shifted to the left, prepared to dodge around him, saying, "Stay back, Evan. Stay. Back."

Evan leaped in front of Cameron, then, blocking Hank's view of her. His hands were raised and his eyes were wide. "Hank, whoa, hold up, buddy. And, uh, Cameron, chill out, because I, uh, I think I, uh, get a say, right? I mean, I get to choose before it comes to blows, am I right? This isn't like some caveman thing where one of you drags me off by my hair. So come on guys, give me a minute, let's take a breath, and—"

"Choose," Hank said at the exact same moment as Cameron. Neither had taken their eyes from the other, both in stances ready to fight. "Choose now."

"Okay, well, okay—I choose, well, I'm sorry, and I hope you don't take this the wrong way, but—"

"Choose!"

"Hank! I choose Hank. Just, both of you, relax, breathe in, breathe out. Let it go with love. Let it go. Just...wow. Now, that? *That* was scary for a minute."

Cameron glared at Hank and turned her back, saying over her shoulder, "I'll take Allison, then. A perfectly good second choice."

Allison glanced nervously between Hank, Evan, and Cameron, and then looked over her shoulder at the shaking applicants who had not been chosen, and said, "Are you sure? You don't think that maybe Maria, or Andy...?"

Cameron sighed. "It was nice meeting you, Allison. Best wishes." She glared at Hank and muttered, "Get back to your territory and stay there. You're on my list, asshole."

Hank didn't bother to answer. Evan stood next to him now, staring at him, and saying, "So, okay, then. Wow. Totally unexpected. But, hey. Cool. I'm happy. Are you happy? I'm really happy. Um, so...what do we do now?"

Hank looked at him. "What do you think, Captain? We screw."

✦   ✦   ✦

DAVID WASN'T SURPRISED when cheers erupted from nearly

everyone in the station the moment that Hank had hollered "Challenge." As the days had passed, it'd become more and more clear that Hank and Evan had a connection, and everyone had started to root for them, even the guys who'd originally lamented that Hank didn't seem interested enough in women's breasts.

David had found it impossible to deny them the fun of watching the final episodes together in the station break room. For a while, there had been some Team Evan vs Team Allison going on, but when it came down to it, David was proud of his little station for dropping their own wish to live vicariously for a desire to see Hank with the best match for him.

When Hank had declared that he wasn't taking an Omega, the mood in the room had plummeted, and there had even been a few tears from Chantal.

The word 'Challenge' made the entire room erupt with excitement. No one seemed to have any doubt that Hank would win the fight. Anyone who had worked with Hank knew that he was nearly unstoppable when he had what he wanted in his sights.

When Evan chose Hank, there was banging on the tables, yelling, and hooting. The only asshole who seemed to have a problem with it had kept his mouth shut and left the room quickly. David made mental note to keep an eye on him in the future. Bigotry wasn't something he would tolerate in his station.

David's cell phone rang. He answered, plugging his other ear in an attempt to hear over the celebration.

"Dad? Did you see that, Dad?" Charles asked.

"I sure did, kiddo."

"That was just so…*cool!*"

David laughed a little, but he wasn't so sure. It'd been dangerous, and it'd been a close call, but cool? David thought that was a bit much.

"Hey, Dad. How *do* two guys screw?"

David choked, sputtered, and snapped, "None of your business! Do your homework and go to bed!"

He hung up the phone and closed his eyes.

God, Hank and that Evan Vaughn kid were going to *screw*. He absolutely did not need to think about that.

CHAPTER THIRTEEN

IT WASN'T QUITE as simple as that, of course. They had interviews to do, questions to answer, and that all took far too long, working Hank's already frazzled nerves.

"So, Evan, what you're saying is that the night when Hank came to your room, you still weren't sure that he was going to choose you."

Evan squeezed Hank's hand and said for the third time in as many minutes, "Dude, you were there. I never thought he was going to choose me. Even at the end."

"Hank, was that played for ratings, or were you really unsure up until the end?"

Hank glared at Warren.

Evan chuckled anxiously, squeezed Hank's fingers again, and said, "Hank doesn't do things for ratings. I'm sure you've figured that out by now."

His nervous laughter filled the space between them, and Hank wanted to knock the microphone out of Warren's hand and get Evan alone, someplace quiet and safe. But Evan was answering another stupid question.

"Well, since you won't tell us about the night he spent in your room, why don't you tell us about that first meeting in the bathroom?"

"Man, I already told you about that, back when it happened," Evan said, his hands shaking as they moved with his words. Hank wanted to grab them from the air and still them, but he didn't, waiting for the right moment to put a stop to all of this.

"Yes, but surely there was more. Was any of this part of your strategy, Evan?"

Evan shook his head, chuckling and vibrating with tension. "Strategy? I, uh, I didn't um, have a strategy? I just sort of…um, what? Hank, what are you…?"

Hank stood up, leaned into the microphone, and said, smiling as sweetly as he could muster, and with the most shit-eating tone possible, "Warren, I think you've got all you're going to get out of us. So, please, get out of my room. Now. And take every last camera and piece of recording equipment with you. I want to be alone now. With my Omega."

Warren smiled lasciviously and if Evan's fingers hadn't been squeezing his own, Hank might have done something to wipe that look off. Instead he sat through the wrap-up sentences and multiple good wishes.

Evan's body shook like a meth addict in detox by the time the door shut on Warren's back.

Hank secured the locks, checked the peephole, checked the windows, and used his Alpha senses to scan the place for anything he might have missed, and found nothing. It was over. The television aspect was behind him.

Now…now he just had a vibrating, nervous, goofy hippie kid, who was supposed to center him through moments a lot more dangerous than this, about to fall apart in front of him.

"I'm not going to ravish you, Captain," Hank said, leaning against the desk opposite the bed where Evan sat shaking like a leaf.

"I know. I mean, of course not. I mean…yeah. I want to do this, and um, I've wanted it for a long time. I jerked off a lot thinking about you the last week or two. And you'd think I was a virgin the way I'm acting, but, don't worry, I've had plenty of experience—"

"Don't talk about that," Hank said. "Not right now."

"Right. Territorial. Bordering on para—"

Hank scoffed. "It's not that I can't handle the idea that you've been with other people, Evan," Hank lied. "It's just not very…romantic."

Evan broke into a broad smile, his eyes taking on a soft, amused glow. "Aha, I knew it. A secret bent toward romance and traditional cultural demonstrations of love and commitment. Very common, actually, for Alphas to want to reflect their cultural mores in these ways, especially in their relationships with their Omega. Historically, many Alphas have married, even in same-sex pairings, for the—"

"We're not getting married."

"Right. Well, I mean, not now or anything! But maybe someday…or maybe never, but, yeah. I see what you're saying, Hank," Evan rambled, looking more unsure than Hank liked.

"Hey, Evan. Who's the Omega here?" Hank asked, crossing his arms over his chest, and waiting for Evan to get the hint.

"Oh…oh, right. Me. I'm the Omega." Evan tucked his hair behind his ears and chuckled again. He cleared his throat and said more firmly, "I guess we should get started."

Hank thought that was a good idea. He'd been feeling restless all day, and since choosing Evan as his Omega, he'd been half-hard and riding increasingly intense waves of lust, each rush stronger than the last. Everything about Evan from his voice, to his quick-moving hands, to the way his blood sounded in his veins was gorgeous, perfect, and all Hank's now. His dick grew even harder.

"Are you nervous, Hank?" Evan asked. "It's normal to be nervous your first time. I'm sure you never thought you'd be here with a guy, right?" Evan was babbling again. "You don't have to be nervous because it'll be easy like—easy like, um, all that's coming to mind is Sunday morning, but that's an awful song, man, and I don't want it stuck in my head for the duration of our lovemaking. So, well, the Aborigines of Australia have a saying—"

Hank smelled the shift in Evan, heard his heart pounding like mad in his chest, as Hank pushed away from the desk to cover Evan's mouth with his hand. Evan's breath puffed against the side of his palm, and his eyes grew bright and definitely a little scared.

"Shh," Hank soothed. "It's me, Captain. I'm not gonna hurt you. I'd never hurt you."

Evan's lips were soft against his palm, and Hank felt the distinct press of them against his skin as Evan kissed his hand. Hank let go of Evan's mouth, and stared at it. Soft, red, wet lips, open and Hank gazed at them as Evan said, "I know, man. I've just never done this before."

Hank tore his eyes from Evan's lips and looked into his eyes, saying, "I thought you said—"

"I've had sex with men, yeah, but I've never bonded with an Alpha. I've read about it, studied it, heard firsthand accounts from Omegas about their experiences during classes in the training academy, so, essentially, I've prepared myself in every way, but…I've never done it. And it's kind of a big commitment. I've, uh, never been so good at those. I'm…heh, well, Hank, I'm kind of terrified."

Hank ran his hand along Evan's cheek, the skin sandpaper rough under the stubble, and then baby-sweet smooth at his cheekbone. He tucked a free strand of Evan's hair behind his ear, and then buried his fingers in the twisting, soft curls. His fingertips discovered the bristle of Evan's hair as it pressed out of his scalp, and then Hank cupped his hand there, feeling the curve of Evan's skull against his palm. "Do you still want to do this, Captain?"

"Yeah. I do. And I'm happy it's you. I've wanted you to know how I feel, but I didn't want to tell you. I thought, if nothing else, we'd be friends."

"We're going to be so much more than friends," Hank growled softly.

"Yeah." Evan licked his lips. His eyes dilated and he blinked slowly. "Do you think you'll shift? It's okay if you shift."

"I won't shift. Probably."

Evan whispered, "You shifted last time we…"

"If I shift this time, it'll be a good shift," Hank said. "Like coming home. If it happens, just stay with me like last time. I've chosen you, and I'd never hurt you."

"Right. I'll try to remember that when the fur pops out and the, uh, teeth…" Evan waved his hand around anxiously. "I do want this. I want you. I want you so bad, Hank."

Hank smiled gently. "So, you've studied this. What do we do first?"

Evan's voice was rough and breathless as he babbled, "I think you should probably start by kissing me. Traditionally in our culture that's the way sex is initiated, and it seems like as good a place as any. Though, of course, if you feel—"

Hank leaned in, closing his eyes as his lips touched Evan's. He groaned, the perfection of his mouth shuddering through him with all the power of truth. And then the sensations took him over.

Salty, soft, hungry, wet. Slippery tongue and sweet spit, too. God, he needed more. So much more. Pushing Evan down and back, his hands slid beneath Evan's shirt. Buttons undone. Off, off, off – there! Yeah, there was Evan's sweet skin. He buried his face against Evan's hairy chest. More hair, warmth and scent. And now, now…this is good, yes, this was almost enough. He needed to just…

Shove down Evan's jeans and boxer briefs, and God, perfect. Soft-hard, velvet, uncut—of course, uncut—and in his hand, in his hand, *in his hand*.

Guttural noises of want and need poured out of him. An incredible *pushing* need consumed him, and he took Evan's mouth, again, all wet and warm. Happiness like he'd never known surrounded him. He grounded himself in it and pushed into it like a bear plunging into his forest home. And it was all Evan.

Evan under him, moving.

Evan's breath in his ear, panting, wanting, "Hank, please. Yes, Hank. Touch me more."

Kissing Evan's throat, Hank slipped his hand lower. He jerked Evan's cock like he did his own, fast and hard, wanting to feel Evan's pleasure erupt. Wanting to smell it.

"Come for me," Hank ordered, his fur pressing against his skin, and his claws stinging the tips of his fingers. But he held them back. "Come for me," he growled.

Evan tensed under him, whimpering and then breaking apart. Overwhelming! Delicious! It was all over, everywhere—salty, sea-smell, baking-soda-sharp. It was wet, sticky, and sloppy, and now slicking Evan's cock. Good. So damn good.

"Hank," Evan's voice panted in his ear. "Hank, now you. *Now you.*"

Hank grunted, shook his head, and backed his senses down from the ecstatic communion with Evan's skin, scent, and beauty. He was hard, achingly hard, and he lay half on top of Evan, his hips moving against Evan's leg frantically. He could come, if he wanted to let go, he could come.

But he slipped his hand up and down Evan's cock again, watching it jerk in his hand, oversensitive and tender. He took a moment to let himself fully accept what he'd been too absorbed to process before. He'd kissed a guy, kissed Evan, and jerked him off. Evan's come was on his hand, white and getting sticky now. He opened up his senses again, adding taste on top of smell, and he smiled as his cock jerked in response.

"Now you," Evan said again, peering up at Hank with open, honest eyes that tugged at him, like a hook deep inside. "C'mon Hank."

Hank lifted up, wiped his hand on the bedspread, and then pulled at Evan's pants until they were completely off. He shucked Evan's socks, and pushed his shirt away, leaving him naked and spread out before him.

Evan breathed heavily. His eyes were dilated, soft pools of blue light. Hank didn't think Evan was beautiful. He was too masculine for that word, all hair and lean muscles and thick, male edges. But Hank couldn't remember ever feeling so fucking turned-on, or so fucking excited in his life, and he wasn't trancing. He was staying right there, right there on the bed with Evan. Who was gorgeous, not beautiful.

Perfectly, deliciously, gorgeous.

Hank's hands trembled when he reached out to grab Evan's hips, dragging him down the bed, positioning him how he needed him—legs spread, knees up. No thoughts, just need, and an instinct he couldn't deny. He shoved Evan's legs higher, exposing his ass, and then he was there. He pressed his mouth against Evan's shivering, hot, intensely scented asshole, and as Hank licked and sucked, Evan's voice arched up like his body.

Hank wanted more, was *starved* for more. His tongue pressed inside, licking; it tasted primal and desperate. He shifted his hold from Evan's legs to his hips, holding him down on the bed. He overrode his Omega's shaking, jumping, twitching body, and gloried in the sensation of Evan's heels pressing hard against his shoulders. Evan twisted under the work of his tongue. He warbled, wet, loud and crazy, and Hank loved it, absorbed it, took in his Omega's noises and assimilated them into his cells, his being, making Evan part of his core.

Evan became incoherent, words and noises came in a stream of sound. Hank held his hips steady, only relaxing his hold enough for Evan to rock his hips gently, soothing himself with the rhythm, until he was whispering, "Okay, okay, I can take it like this. I can handle this, oh, God, oh, God, Hank, Hank." His voice went choked and overwhelmed.

Hank gripped him tightly again, stopped the rocking, and sucked, licked, and kissed Evan's asshole fast and hard again. Evan bucked against him, his hands pushing at Hank's head. His feet shoved at Hank's shoulders, as his voice lifted in a shaking wail. Hank backed off, listening to the hectic rush of Evan's pulse and the thudding of his heart, and then leaned in, kissing Evan's quivering asshole sweetly.

He sat back on his heels when he felt Evan surrender to the pleasure, collapsing against the bed in a shaking heap and sobbing with joy. He met Evan's wet and completely wild eyes then and reached for the lube left conveniently out on the bedside table. Hank unbuttoned his pants, shoved them down around his hips, and poured lube onto his cock.

Evan's heart rate sped up. "That's big."

"Yeah," Hank agreed, slicking himself thoroughly. Then he met Evan's gaze again, saying, "Ready, Captain?"

Evan swallowed and nodded, suddenly silent. Hank felt the waves of heat from Evan's skin, saw the flush rush up his body, and knew that Evan wanted him. His eyes landed on Evan's cock, smiling to see a pearl of precum on the head, and drops of Evan's prior load drying in places on this stomach.

"C'mon, Hank," Evan whispered, his voice cracked and gruff.

Hank didn't need more. He ran his hand over his cock, making sure the lube was everywhere and then rubbed his slick hand over Evan's asshole. The still clenching pucker was a tease under his fingertips, and, then, shouldering Evan's legs, he moved into place. He lined up his cock and groaned, pushing in and down.

Evan moaned, relaxed, and seemed to *open*. And, fuck, Hank hadn't known how that tight little hole was going to take him, but it was. It was incredible, mind blowing; it was fucking *religious* how damn good Evan felt. How tight, how hot, how fucking amazing. The clench and the pull of Evan's ass on his cock stole his breath. He groaned and sank in. No, Evan *pulled* him in.

"God, Captain," Hank said, unable to pull his eyes away from where his dick disappeared into Evan with slow, deliberate strokes, deeper and deeper.

"Hank," Evan's voice cut through to him, and Hank darted a glance up. "Your shirt." Evan's voice was soft, kind of stunned, and Hank stared at him, caught between focusing his attention on his cock's tight, sweet press into Evan's body, and the need to understand what Evan was saying.

"Take off your shirt," Evan said again.

Hank tried to shake himself. His cock was halfway in Evan's ass, and his shirt? Take off his shirt?

"I wanna feel you, man," Evan said. "Please."

Hank groaned, every instinct telling him to push on ahead, but he gritted his teeth together and pulled out, hearing Evan take in a sharp, shocked breath. Hank yanked his shirt over his head, pushed his pants off, and threw them all aside.

Then Evan sat up, grabbed Hank by the shoulders, and murmured, "Kiss me. Like this—"

Oh, yeah.

He whimpered, loving the way Evan kissed. He loved the taste of his lips and wet tongue, and adored Evan's hands on him, stroking his back. Evan's hips rocked up, and there—*there*, Evan's cock was hard again, and leaking precum. He could smell it and feel the slide of it against his skin.

Hank groaned. "Now?"

Evan cocked his hips up, and Hank pulled back enough to add more lube to his cock. Then he aimed and pushed inside. Throwing his head back, he growled, the bear inside rumbling with joy.

"Fuck me," Evan said urgently. "Make me yours."

The bear roared, and Hank shouted with it. And this time the fuck was even. Evan moved beneath him like a writhing, hungry animal, and his grip on Hank's arms left finger-sized points of pain that grounded him. The sensation of plunging again and again into Evan's hot, twisting body was almost overwhelming, but Hank didn't stop. Instead, he focused on Evan's eyes, open and hot, so fucking hot that they burned Hank with their heat and made him tremble.

Hank kissed him again. Wet, messy, good. Stubble scratched over stubble, shocking him a little. The piercing pleasure left him groaning and fucking into Evan's ass hard, with a wildness barely restrained. Fur pressed against his skin. Claws stung his fingertips. But he held it back, focusing on Evan's scent and sounds to stay human, to fuck into the man who would save him from himself.

He closed his eyes and buried his face in Evan's neck. "Love this," he groaned. "I love it."

"Love you," Evan answered, and Hank teared up.

He kissed Evan's neck, willing his emotions to pour into his Omega as he made love to him. He reveled in the scratch of stubble against his forehead, and the scratch of leg hair on his back where Evan's legs hooked around his waist. Even more hair rubbed against his stomach and chest, and he loved it, he fucking loved it all. He loved Evan. "I love you, too."

Evan clutched him close and spasmed around his cock, making them both cry out in pleasure. Hank let himself get lost in that sweet abrasion, and he lived there with each thrust and tug, until he felt as though he'd never make his way out of it again. Focusing on Evan's pounding heart, he drew back from the edge of a trance and moaned. Then his focus slid away to catch on the throb of Evan's pulse beating rapidly against Hank's cock when he shoved deep and held still.

"Harder," Evan muttered. "Make me come again."

Roaring, Hank let go, lost his grip, and with his Alpha senses dove deep into the sensations. Deeper and deeper.

It was hot, tight, good, and gripping, *oh, oh, sweetheart, oh, Captain, goddammit*, and Evan squirmed hard under him, then yelled. The scent of Evan's cum pummeled Hank again, layered with Evan's wild moans, and…*fuck*, everything was so damn *good*. More than good. Perfect. Blissful. He pushed hard on Evan's legs, shoving them higher, getting in deeper, and then he was lost again.

Hot, tight, sweat, slick, heat, and….

Falling!

Soaring and shaking!

Fuck! *Fuck!* Spurting and coming so hard that he blacked out.

Hank was caught in a loop of pleasure, trapped in a moment of ecstasy. It enveloped him in deep rightness, before it ended suddenly and completely. The loss of such intense feeling was both a disappointment and a relief. Hank collapsed on Evan's hairy chest, trembling and shaking, breathing hard and fast. His cock still jerked in Evan's tight ass, spasms of aftershock that twitched him like a landed fish.

Holy shit, fucking Evan was beyond good. It was sheer divinity.

Distantly, Hank heard Evan talking. Yes, he was talking and

talking, while stroking Hank's back. Hank shuddered, groaned, and moved his head to kiss Evan's neck. Evan's voice went on, still saying something, and rambling on. It warmed Hank's heart and he drifted on the sound comfortably. Evan's syllables rose and fell all around him, and Hank could almost pluck them out of the air and eat them for lunch.

Pulling free of Evan's ass was a necessary misery, though. Hank felt the loss like a visceral thing and he almost shoved back inside. But instead soothed Evan when he hissed with pain, a moment of exhaled breath and a grimace, that Hank regretted. He kissed Evan's cheek, his collarbone, and his throat.

Then Evan was talking some more. The sounds were a blanket of comfort and perfection, and Hank wrapped himself in them, though he was too blissed out to make a lick of sense out of them.

Collapsing again with his head on Evan's chest, he relaxed for the first time possibly ever. His muscles unwound, his breathing slowed, and he smiled as he let the bear inside surface just a little. When fur sprouted on his neck, Evan's hand didn't slow in its rubbing; instead, it began moving in slow circles over the bristles while he continued to talk and talk.

Hank soaked in the scent of his Omega's juices, and he exulted in the sensation of complete acceptance. He let more of his bear rise to the top—his sleepy bear, his comfortable bear, and, yes, his happy bear. His claws pushed slowly through his fingertips and he raked them gently over Evan's fragile skin, taking them over the softness of his belly and leaving small marks behind.

Evan's heartbeat rose briefly and his voice pitched up higher as anxiety pierced him, but when Hank nuzzled him, pressing his half shifted face against Evan's neck, he calmed again.

"Tickles, man," Hank made out, and he ran his nails over

Evan's belly one more time, slightly harder, leaving strong, red stripes behind without breaking skin. Marking his Omega. Then he drifted his hand lower, resting his claws against Evan's tender inner thighs. He scratched more gently there, but still left his mark.

Evan's heart raced, his cock rose, and Hank laughed against his hairy chest. "I love you," he muttered again, very carefully running his claws over Evan's balls, smiling as Evan's cock spasmed and a small load of cum shot out.

"Fuck," Evan hissed. "That was…fuck."

Holy Christ, was his bear content. Proud. Satisfied as fuck. He held Evan's balls in his hand and kept his claws just touching the skin. He'd fucked a man. He'd fucked *Evan*. He'd fucked his *Omega*. And, damn, it had been worth the wait.

Evan rattled on, even as his cock woke and grew fatter under Hank's very careful claws. "…maybe it's like a delayed reaction? I mean, I thought it was supposed to be instantaneous but I don't feel any different. Every Omega I've interviewed, and every report that I've read said they felt the difference immediately following coitus. Even during coitus. Some described it as a blossoming, others as a click, or a shift of some nature, but I didn't feel anything. Did you, Hank? Do you feel different?"

Hank felt different, all right. He felt bone-deep sated, exhausted, and deliriously relaxed. His bear was in ecstasy. He'd found his mate, his home. "Hmm?"

"The bonding. I think something went wrong. I don't feel any different."

Hank tried to clear his head. Pulling his fur and claws back in, he ran his hand down Evan's chest again, encountering the sticky remnants of Evan's cum. He rubbed it against Evan's skin, noting the texture of it, the slippery feel of it on his fingers. "Feels good," Hank said. "I feel good."

Evan chuckled. "Yeah, I bet you do. 'Fucked brains out. Feel good.' But, come on, Caveman, this is important. Did we bond?"

Hank propped up on one arm enough to look down at Evan's face and scanned the length of his body. What he'd just done and what he'd just felt had been like nothing he'd ever imagined or wanted before. The primitive urge that had overtaken him and led him to fold Evan nearly in half as he'd fucked him had been uncontrollable.

Wallowing in his senses without drowning, exulting in them, nearly rolling in them, like an animal in the wild who marked themselves with the most intense scents of their home, claiming it as they wore it, had been perfection.

Thrusting into Evan's ass, holding him down and taking in his every noise, every movement, knowing everything Evan felt even while losing himself completely, tasting Evan's pleasure, tasting the moment he gave in to orgasm, feeling and smelling his bliss? Beyond his wildest dreams of union. He felt a strong stirring inside, an urge to do what they'd just done again.

"Maybe we were wrong..." Evan said, his voice tense and confused. "What if we were wrong?"

"We're bonded," Hank said, throwing his leg over Evan's body. He realized that he knew the location of every mole and freckle, the size and shape of every scar on Evan's body, and though he'd felt completely gone in the midst of it, he'd actually been more present than he'd ever been in his life.

"Are you sure? I don't feel anything? All Omegas have reported—"

"We're bonded," Hank repeated.

"Really? Because—"

"We're bonded, Captain. Stop worrying about it."

"I don't know, Hank. I mean, like I said, I don't feel any different. I think I would notice if I'd made some kind of significant shift in my consciousness, and I was looking for it, you know, waiting for it. I was hoping to make some good notes on the experience, maybe shed some light on the bonding process itself. Like does it happen at orgasm, or penetration, or…"

"Captain—"

"I don't feel any different, Hank!" Evan exclaimed.

Hank, with a mild bit of frustration rising, said, "Wait until you get up and start moving around. Your ass will tell you otherwise."

"Hey, man, this is *not* a joke." Evan sounded on the verge of panic.

"Evan," Hank said, keeping his voice as level as possible, sensing that now was not the time to lose his patience. "Okay, you don't feel different. What, exactly, are you supposed to feel?"

"It's not the same for every Omega, but most report a physical sensation accompanying a mental shift, and afterwards they just know things, like what their Alpha needs and wants, and how to keep them from trancing, and what they—"

"Captain, you've always known what I need, right?" Hank said, softly, trailing his fingers through Evan's chest hair. Hell, just moments before Evan had passively allowed Hank in half-shifted form to mark his body and touch his balls, because he'd known, somehow, that Hank needed it.

Evan's hand came up to still his fingers. "Have I? Have I really, Hank?"

"What do I need right now?" Hank asked.

"I don't know! I mean, I could guess. I'd say…well, you need me to calm down, focus, and stay present. You need me to make you laugh. You need me to…roll over and let you fuck me again? Really, Hank? *Really?* That's what you want? In case you haven't noticed, I'm sort of freaking out here, man."

Hank made a soft, reassuring sound, and said, "Well, if you

think I didn't do it right to begin with, Captain, there's no harm in trying again." He thrust his hard cock against Evan a little. "And, in case you haven't noticed, yeah, that's exactly what I want—what I need…"

Evan snorted, his eyes glowing with amusement. Hank could smell the shift in Evan's mental state, the way the acrid panic dissipated, replaced by sweet amusement and musky lust.

Evan said, "So, I take it that you don't mind my man-parts after all? Or that I'm not very leggy or blonde?"

"I can say that didn't even cross my mind," Hank whispered and nudged Evan's shoulder, turning him onto his stomach, taking long, deep sniffs along Evan's skin, pressing soft kisses along his shoulders as he climbed between Evan's strong thighs. He felt and smelled and tasted Evan relaxing, letting go entirely of his panic and fear. After spreading more lube on his cock, Hank pushed into Evan's ass again, groaning at the clenching heat, resting his forehead on Evan's trembling shoulders.

"Do you feel different yet, Captain?" Hank asked, panting as he thrust deep and held himself in tight.

"God, Hank," Evan whispered into the pillow he was clench-ing in both hands. "You're big, man."

"It doesn't hurt," Hank said, and somehow he knew it didn't, knew without any doubt that Evan was only aching with pleasure.

"It's good," Evan said softly. "Really good."

He poured his own feelings and sensations into the bond he felt between them. He let the bear send his pleasure and posses-sive devotion through too. Evan whimpered and trembled all over. "Oh, man, yeah—okay, um…wow."

"Different?" Hank asked.

"Yeah," Evan said, rocking his hips back, making Hank grab him to hold him down. Hank could tell he liked that, felt the submissive thrill of being physically manhandled through their bond. "Oh, um, yeah. So damn different. Fuck, Hank. Just—oh, God…"

Hank didn't wait for more, rocking hard into Evan's ass, giving himself over to pleasure and connection again, knowing that Evan was there to keep him from ever getting too lost in their physical bliss. He was so damn grateful for Evan that he could cry, but instead he just fucked Evan more softly, taking his time, drawing it out. He loved Evan's body twisting under his, the scratch of body hair, and the smooth softness of flesh. He grasped Evan's fingers in his own as they moved together.

The scent of Evan's cum smashed into him, and he cried out in joy. He fucked him harder, and the pleasured wail rising from Evan vibrated along Hank's skin, trembled in his hair, and washed him with Evan's ecstasy. Hank pressed on, his cock plunging into the perfection of Evan's body—so tight and so welcoming.

He struggled just a breath away from heaven, his skin pulling tight and his balls drawing up. And when he came, trancing hard on so much pleasure, Evan was there for him, holding him, and pulling him out of the loop of feeling.

Bringing him home.

CHAPTER FOURTEEN

After Hank brought Evan to a third very hard, very loud orgasm, having taken over an hour to do it, there was no more fussing from Evan about whether or not they were bonded. Instead, Evan sat in a freshly showered, slightly damp, exhausted, robe-covered lump on the floor by the half-open door to the patio, drinking tea and staring out toward the ocean.

Hank lounged on the newly made bed gazing in Evan's direction. Heartbeat steady, pulse smooth, and breathing deep and easy, Evan didn't seem anxious anymore. If anything, he seemed very relaxed, very comfortable, though Hank thought they should eat soon. Hank could smell a slight acrid scent, something he recognized as hunger beginning to taint Evan's breath. He took a moment to be amazed at the level of attunement he was experiencing with Evan, how he now felt automatically aware of the smallest details, the quietest shift…like he knew that Evan was going to talk now.

"I should write down some notes," Evan said, not sounding very eager.

"No rush," Hank replied, resisting the impulse to drag Evan onto the bed so he could lick his asshole some more. Evan was tired and needed a rest.

"It's just nothing like I thought it would be. I thought it would be…" Evan trailed off and took a sip of his tea before sighing. "I just feel really raw. Exposed."

Hank didn't know what to say. He felt whole, warm, satisfied, and happy. Happier than he'd ever felt in his life. Hearing that Evan felt otherwise, his heart tightened, his throat clenched, and he focused on Evan completely, scanning him up and down, looking for something to fix. But it was as it was before—Evan was calm and relaxed, his body uncoiled and limp, and his heart rate peaceful.

"Hank, stop," Evan said softly. "I'm fine. Yeah, I feel raw, but it's like…I don't know, like I've been completely torn apart and put back together again in the most intensely pleasurable way possible. I feel sort of vulnerable, like a new person." He paused, evaluated his own words and said, "I guess it *is* like what the other Omegas reported. Just not what I thought. It's hard to explain, man."

Hank watched him closely, still not sure it was okay. Not sure that Evan was okay, even though every single thing about him, everything Hank could tell from the bond that fit him more tightly than his own skin, was perfect in every way.

"Yeah, man," Evan said, smiling in his direction. "Perfect is a good word for it." Hank wondered if Evan realized what he'd done. If he did, he wasn't showing it, continuing to talk without stopping, "Yeah, I feel taken apart and remade to fit you perfectly."

Hank tensed his jaw, something about that not sitting right with him. Evan remade? That wasn't what he wanted.

Evan held up his hands, saying, "No, no, it's good. It's okay. No, man, no…don't get that way, all right?" Evan's eyes glowed with his usual open honesty as he said, "It's perfect."

Hank didn't know what to say, and still feeling uncertain that Evan was still *Evan*, he moved over to pull him up from the floor. He shut the patio door, opened Evan's robe, and ran his hands down his body. He wanted to check again, make sure he still felt good, make sure that he hadn't been remade in any way, shape, or form.

Evan chuckled and pushed his hands away, closing his robe again, and turning his back. "I can't go again, man. Not yet. Feed me, let me rest, and then we'll see. Right now, though, you're out of luck, my love. Out. Of. Luck."

Hank could smell Evan's arousal, and knew if he pushed it even a little that he'd have him begging again. Instead, Hank picked up the phone and dialed room service, smiling when Evan grabbed it from his hand and started ordering food like a starving man who'd just been on a twenty-mile hike uphill both ways.

✦ ✦ ✦

HOURS LATER, HANK woke up to the smell of pencil lead and he cracked his eyes open to see Evan shifting restlessly at the desk as he scribbled in a journal. He was muttering again. "Omega's reports are unreliable…no, not unreliable…tainted. Tainted by the individual nature of the experience…and expectations, culturally programmed expectations…"

Hank listened as Evan scribbled on and on, feeling the moment when Evan realized that he was being watched. He was gratified that Evan didn't stop his writing to acknowledge him, not for several minutes anyway. When he finally turned around, he smiled and said, "Sleep well?"

"Taking notes, Captain?"

"Anthropologist, Hank. It's what I do."

"How detailed are those notes?"

"Detailed," Evan replied. He held his body very still, almost defensive, and Hank realized that whatever he'd written down, he suspected Hank wouldn't be pleased with it. Hank also knew why.

"Who's going to read it?"

Evan shrugged. "I don't know yet. It's important information. It could help future generations of Omegas and Alphas to understand the intricacies of bonding."

"By making copious and detailed notes about our sex life?" Hank asked. "Did you put in there how many times we fucked and in what positions and how much you liked each one?"

Evan's mouth dropped open a little, his eyes wide, and he waited a long time before he said, "Yes. Yes to all of that, Hank. It's all relevant to the bonding process, and it's important for a myriad of academic reasons. But also to let future generations of Omega and Alpha pairs know that no matter the cultural mores they've been born into, the sexual aspect is nonnegotiable, intense, natural, shameless, and epic."

"Epic?"

"Yeah, epic," Evan said, crossing his arms over his chest.

"Can't argue with that," Hank said, his dick already waking up to the idea of another epic event on the horizon. He hadn't been this easy to arouse since he was a kid, since he'd been little Hank with his hands under the covers, thinking about Silvia in the apple tree.

"So." Evan said, defensively.

"So?" Hank replied.

"You're going to let me do this?" He sounded surprised.

"You can write it down all you want, Captain, so long as you safeguard the journals with your life. But when it comes time to show them to someone, we'll have to talk."

"So, you're delaying the argument then," Evan said.

"Evan, you're an anthropologist. You do what you do. I can't stop you. In fact, I like it. As for giving my consent to have my sex life published in some anthropological journal? That's nonnegotiable. I don't consent. Over my dead body."

Evan seemed to ponder this for a moment, and then he

smiled. The expression was wicked but completely determined. "No problem, Hank. I'll just mark them as only publishable posthumously."

Hank blinked, paused, and took in Evan's single-minded expression. Posthumously, huh? Maybe. He'd be dead after all. Who gave a damn what people thought of him then? He shrugged, unwilling to debate it now or probably ever.

"C'mere," Hank said, pushing aside the covers to show Evan what he had in store for him.

"Oh, no. No, no, man." Evan shook his head. "My ass is totally out of commission for today."

"Who said anything about your ass?" Hank asked. "We have mouths, don't we?"

"Oh!" Evan grinned. "Oh, well! When you put it like that…."

Hank half sat up as Evan stood, shucked his robe, and crossed to the bed. Evan shoved Hank back down, smiling naughtily, and Hank grinned, too, when he realized what Evan had in mind.

Evan's thick cock in his mouth might have kept him from saying just how good his own felt stuffed into Evan's, but he could tell that Evan still got the message.

CHAPTER FIFTEEN

HANK FELT THE cameras on them as they walked through the airport, could hear the snick of the paparazzi taking their photo. It was bizarre. Hank and Evan's bags had been sent on ahead, except for Evan's small backpack that he kept fiddling around in, trying to find a notebook or something.

Hank sensed her before her saw her. Cameron stood at the snack shop by the escalators, a magazine in hand, and her eyes on Hank. He nodded curtly to her, and she lifted her chin in a cold acknowledgment.

Evan, who had pulled a notebook from his backpack with a triumphant noise just moments before, snorted under his breath at the tension that arced in the space between Hank and the other Alpha. "Do you think maybe we should be polite? Go on over and say hello?"

Hank glared at Evan.

"Okay, then," Evan said, rocking onto his toes, hands shoved into his pockets, and the notebook tucked under his arm. He studied Cameron, who was now making a very large show of *not* looking at them. "So, what about Cameron, huh, Hank? Some sexual tension between you two, don't you think?"

"I think you're insane, Evan," Hank gritted out.

"Oh, come on. She's smart, tough, and another Alpha. If the two of you were to…" He made a fucking motion with his hands. "Just think, you could have little Alphas running around."

"Think you're pretty funny, do you?"

Evan laughed, his entire body bending with his chuckles. "Yeah. Yeah, I do."

"Well, you're not."

Evan made a face that indicated he thought Hank was a giant party-pooper. "Oh, ho. Someone can't take a joke. Which, you know, makes the two of you a lot alike. And you know what they say about people who are a lot alike?" Evan waggled his eyebrows suggestively.

"You're forgetting your physics, Captain. Opposites attract."

Evan's smile was happy and genuine. "Yeah, that's true. Just look at us, man. Complete opposites. I'm only saying, if you wanted to explore the vee scenario, she might be a good bet."

Hank clenched his jaw to prevent himself from grabbing Evan and pulling him into a restroom to fuck him blind. He shook his head, trying to shake off the primitive possessive urge, and gritted out, "I don't share well."

"Right, it'd be the vee. You and her, me and you, and never me and her."

Hank growled softly under his breath and clenched his fists. He felt fur prickling at his neck and his teeth growing longer. Evan put his hand on his arm immediately, exasperated amusement underlying his voice as he said, "Calm down, big guy, it was just a suggestion. I was just letting you know that I'd be open to that if that's what *you* wanted."

"I don't," Hank said, his jaw aching now.

"Gotcha," Evan said. "I hear you. Moving on then." Evan gripped Hank's arm firmly and steered them on ahead.

Hank had calmed down by the time they got to the VIP waiting area. They still had an hour before their flight. Hank flipped through a book and double-checked that he had earplugs for takeoff.

Evan listened to some music on headphones with a lot of

drums, fuzzy guitar, and lyrics about being someone's sugarcane, and that's all Hank could take before he'd purposely tuned it out. He was exhausted after weeks of constant observation and stress, and several days of near ceaseless sex. He closed his eyes and drowsed a bit, leaning his head against the wall, dropping in and out of a light sleep.

"Hank, man, I'm gonna go get some peanuts and a Coke and look for some magazines for the plane. Want anything?"

Hank lifted a hand dismissively and slipped back toward sleep. His dreams had been weird the last few nights. He'd even had one where the bear mounted the wolf and fucked him. He'd woken up hard and vaguely disturbed until Evan had rolled over and said, "Man, I just had a dream that I was a wolf, and I got fucked by a bear. What do you think that *means*?" And then Hank had showed him just what it meant.

Hank didn't even realize that he'd been trailing Evan with his Alpha senses until he sat up, suddenly quite alert, and ready to move.

"Hey," Evan said. "Good to see you, Cameron."

"You, too, Evan." Cameron's voice was quiet, but she must have known that Hank could hear her. "You look exhausted. Is your Alpha not attending to your basic needs?"

Evan's response made Hank smile. "His very intense attention to my needs is why I look so exhausted."

"Of course," Cameron said, her voice tight.

"Listen," Evan said. "I just wanted you to know, you're awesome and all, but I wouldn't have accepted, even if Hank hadn't chosen me that night. I was gonna have to say no. I wouldn't have been the right Omega for you."

"I guess we'll never know for sure."

"I know for sure." Evan's heart rate was steady. He wasn't at all anxious. Hank waited a little longer. "You know, Cameron, I have a friend at the Omega training program at Spruce. I think you'd like her, and, what's more, I think she'd like you. Here…here's her number. Tell her I said for you to call. Set up a meeting. I'm sure she'd fly to Atlanta. If she's not the one for you, well…she meets a lot of potential Omegas in her position. She might know of someone else. Go on—take it. What do you have to lose?"

When Evan returned with the peanuts and cola, and three magazines tucked under his arm, he smiled and sat next to Hank. "I hope she finds someone, man. She deserves better than what she'll get without an Omega. No one deserves that."

Hank thought about the future he'd avoided when Evan followed him to be on this stupid television show, and he reached out to take Evan's hand. They'd managed to ditch the cameras at the front of the VIP area, but Hank could still feel watching eyes all around. He squeezed Evan's fingers and dropped his hand to point at one of the magazines in Evan's lap.

"The Biggest Sex Scandals of the Year?"

"Yeah, man, the anthropological interest of these magazines should not be underestimated. Did you know that—"

Hank noticed a photo of him and Evan from the night of the finale tucked into the corner of the magazine Evan was about to open. The words beneath read, "Alpha Morrow Has Chosen!"

"Give me that," Hank muttered, snatching it from Evan's hand.

"Haha, oh, yeah, man, apparently we're quite the big deal. We have *fans*. The other Alphas do, too, of course, but apparently we are the surprise hit pairing of the show. Something about our chemistry, I don't know, but it's pretty funny—"

Hank flipped through the magazine until he found the article. As he scanned the pages quickly, his eyes landed on a blurry photo-capture of Evan kissing Fong; the words underneath seared into his brain. "It was thought that Vaughn might end up with Fong—" His heart thumped and his breath felt weird as he sucked it in.

"Oh, hey, man," Evan said, trying to pull the magazine back from him. "Come on, just a little smoochy-smoochy, no big deal, right?"

Hank said nothing, grappling with an urge to hunt down Fong immediately, wherever in the world he might be, and rip his lips off, and his dick, too.

"Look, Hank, read the rest of it. 'It was thought that Evan might end up with Fong, *but his connection with Morrow won out.* See? Nothing to worry about. Everyone knows who I'm with, man, just chill. Jeez, does this hyperactive overreaction fade away soon? 'Cause, man, I've been with a lot of people in my time, and if you're going to end up freaking out every time we run into someone I've schtupped, much less kissed, then we'll have to leave White Edge."

Hank glared fondly at him.

Evan snatched the magazine from Hank's hands and stuffed it into his backpack. He rolled his eyes and muttered under his breath about territorial Alphas, and then opened another magazine he'd picked up. *National Geographic* this time. Hank could nearly hear Evan's thoughts, knew that he was thinking that surely there was nothing in *this* magazine that would set Hank off.

Hank took some deep breaths, listened to Evan's heart, and took in his scent, filtering out the odors of other people in the room.

Evan was *his* Omega, and that didn't change, no matter how many other people...or Alphas...he'd kissed in the past. He could feel Evan sending that message to him in the air between them, the subtle waves of connection that came from the lean of

Evan's body, the gentle kick of his foot against Hank's calf, and the way his eyes dilated when he glanced Hank's way, his pupils opening up to swallow Hank whole, to let him in. Always letting him in.

Hank relaxed, sending his own message to Evan with the release of tension in his body. Evan murmured, "See, man? No big deal."

Hank exhaled a breath and scanned the perimeter of the room, watching as people settled their bags and bought drinks at the bar, listening for anything untoward, sniffing for drugs or other contraband items, and found nothing of concern.

Evan exclaimed about some article he was reading, using his hands to point and jab at the pages as he babbled on about new information on a tribe near the Ganges that he'd spent some time studying. Hank sent his senses out farther in the airport, sorting through the shuffling of feet, the wailing of children, the scent of perfumes, and finally finding what he was looking for.

He settled into his seat and half-listened to Evan and half-followed Cameron's progress through the airport and onto the plane that would take her back home. He hoped Evan's friend could help her. Evan was right. She was a good person, a committed Alpha, and she deserved an Omega just as much as any of them.

Just not his Omega.

No, Evan belonged with him.

✦　　✦　　✦

DAVID ROLLED HIS eyes at the sign that Chantal and Lydia from reception held high in the air when Evan and Hank appeared on the escalators down from the terminal. Hank and his new Omega seemed surprised to find the bunch of them waiting by the baggage conveyor, which was the plan. But the stupid amount of flailing going on was starting to piss David off.

"Leave the man alone," David barked, popping an unlit cigarette into his mouth, cursing the non-smoking policy of the airport's main terminal and baggage claim area.

Hank lifted his chin in grateful acknowledgment of David's efforts, but the women only dispersed when the men pushed forward, offering their hands to shake and passing around manly thumps on the back. David didn't miss Hank's relief that so many of his male co-workers weren't making a big deal about his male Omega.

There was another group there, too, a somewhat larger group, from the university. Apparently, Evan was pretty popular in his academic world, and about two dozen people using three-dollar words were busy clapping Evan on the back, hugging him, and generally manhandling the kid. David could tell that Hank was tense about that, one eye always turned in Evan's direction, and hardly hearing anything that the guys from the station were saying, despite his best efforts.

"We were rooting for you guys," Ben said.

"Yeah, it was just so obvious," Lee volunteered, leaving out any reference to his previous grousing about the lack of ta-tas on Evan.

"Thanks," Hank said, his head turned toward Evan who was laughing about something. David snorted at the goofy expression that flashed over Hank's face when he looked at the kid.

Evan glanced back Hank's direction and there seemed to be a moment where a communication took place, because he nodded a little and then started saying his goodbyes to his friends. David heard him saying, "Yeah, I'll bring him around, man. For sure. I can't wait for you all to really meet him. Thanks for coming out, yeah, wow, you're all so awesome."

Hank broke away from the guys from the station long enough to go over and clasp a few hands from Evan's group, and then the academics dispersed. David took the hint, saying loudly, "Our job here is done. Hank knows we're happy he's home. Now—everyone get the hell out of here."

He wasn't surprised that there was some grumbling about it, especially from the women, but everyone did start to leave, a few stopping to shake Hank's hand again and gaining a fast introduction to Evan in the process. David noted that there were touches between Hank and Evan, but nothing overt, everything casual, but each nudge and press of hand on arm spoke volumes.

"C'mon," said David. "I'll take you home."

"Evan," Hank said, "This is David. David, Evan."

David shook hands with the kid and found that he was nearly vibrating, bouncing on the balls of his feet, his eyes shining with excitement.

"Nice to meet you, David. I've heard a lot about you."

David doubted that.

Evan went on, "And I am honored to be part of your team. I can't wait to get started—"

"Slow down, kiddo," David said. "Why don't you get settled first, spend a week with Hank at home, get that silly look off of both of your faces, and then we'll put you to work."

"A week?" Hank said, incredulous. He hefted his suitcase and Evan followed suit. As they headed out into night, the red and white of car lights flashed past as they crossed the street between the airport proper and the parking lots.

"You should see how you look at each other, Hank. I think a week might be at a minimum. I can't have my top officer distracted by sudden *urges.*"

Hank scoffed and David held up his hand, stemming comments, and then stalked ahead of them both, saying, "I'm telling you now. A week. Get the kid moved in with you. Get settled. Do what you have to do to get all of this out of your system. And then come back to work. We can hold down the fort a little longer."

Hank started to argue, but Evan piped up, "David's probably right, Hank. Things are a little intense right now."

"I can keep my hands off you, Captain," Hank said, obviously irritated.

Evan just laughed, and Hank's annoyance grew. David could hear the bluster beginning, but Evan simply interjected with, "The LAX bathroom, Hank. Twice. *Twice*, man."

Hank made a noise like he wanted to dispute that whatever depraved sexual activity Evan was referencing had actually taken place, but he said nothing at all about it, and instead asked, grumpily, "Where the hell did you park, David? Egypt?"

David replied, "Yes, and I did it just to piss you off."

Evan's laughter undercut Hank's gruff reply, and David smiled.

It was an entertainment age; his ex-wife had been right about that. He glanced at Hank, who had his hand on the back of Evan's neck, shaking him softly in mock irritation.

Yes, for once the bitch had been right. Luckily for Hank.

EPILOGUE

"H ANK, I'VE BEEN thinking," Evan said as they piled the boxes from his apartment into Hank's truck. "At what point, exactly, did you know you were going to choose me?"

Hank groaned, lifting the heaviest box of books up over the lip of the truck bed, dusted his hands off and said, "Why does it matter, Captain? I did and we're here. That's enough, right?"

"Sure, Hank. Yeah," Evan said, but the long-inhaled breath that would precede even more words told Hank that his agreement was lip service. "That's all well and good, man, but here's the thing. I've got this theory. I think that you and I started bonding before we were even aware of it. There's the belief, you know, that bonding takes place during sexual intercourse between an Alpha and an Omega, but there's really no direct evidence that it begins and ends there, Hank."

"Uh-huh," Hank said, lifting the next box into the truck, noticing that Evan was now resting against the bumper, absorbed in his words, moving his hands along to the rhythm of them, and absolutely not helping load his damn boxes into the truck.

"I mean, the Ancient Woods Children and the White Moon people both believed that the Alpha and the Omega had a soul connection, something that is given lip-service even today, and they exploit that aspect during the show, remember? But it isn't really studied or explored too much because it's so out there on the edge, man. Science turns its nose up at it because it isn't based in something that's absolutely concrete and observable."

"Hand me that, Captain," Hank said, indicating the strap to hold the larger boxes in place.

Evan grabbed the lose end of the strap and passed it over to Hank, making a show of pretending to hold the boxes in place while Hank secured the line. "But what we have here, Hank, is a case where we could document at least some of what a beginning bond looks like, some of it with audio and video documentation, even. A bond that began far earlier than the sexual consummation."

"The point, Captain?"

"The point is, Hank, this is a big deal. You and I…well, our bond started early, didn't it? You felt it, even when you didn't know what it was."

Hank shrugged. Sure, he'd felt it and, true, he hadn't known what it was, but most of all he hadn't been willing to find out. His subconscious humiliation at wanting a man had kept him from acknowledging what was obvious to everyone but him.

"Hank, do you know what I think?"

"No idea," Hank said, working the final smaller boxes into the back of the truck.

"I think we started bonding the first time we met."

"In the bathroom. Yeah. I guess."

"No, man, the *first* time we met. Here, in White Edge, at the mixer."

Hank grunted, shifting a big box into a better position. "I didn't even remember you from the mixer, Captain. I still don't."

"Sure you did. And you do! Just not consciously. Remember how you didn't even react to me being in the bathroom, remember how we just clicked together and it worked? That's what I'm talking about, man, that's what I'm thinking! The first time we met here in White Edge you were so shut off to everything, your soul recognized mine, but *you* didn't. And, in a way, it was the same for me."

Hank lifted his brows skeptically. There had long been discussions about Alphas connecting with a specific Omega across lifetimes. But there wasn't a lot of discussion about Omegas connecting with a specific Alpha—though it went unsaid, obviously. He wondered now that he'd never noticed that before, how Alpha-centric it seemed, and yet Evan hadn't even brought that up. The kid was rubbing off on him.

"Well, maybe with less repression and sublimation for me," Evan went on. "I definitely thought about you a lot after I met you at the mixer. I just didn't think I stood a chance getting inside your walls. No one did. But when I saw your name on that list for the show? I'll never forget how I felt in that moment. I just knew I had to go, had to be there, and it was because of you, man, because of having met you." Evan looked up earnestly. "I can't believe that even I was too uptight, though, to realize what that meant."

Hank shook his head. "You've lost me, Captain. What did it mean, exactly?"

"We'd started bonding. It's a *process* Hank, not a moment. Or, well, it can be a moment, sure, but a real bond begins with a process, and that's why you couldn't satisfy yourself with Allison—"

"Let's not talk about that, Captain." It still embarrassed him to think about how consumed he'd been by her when his precious Omega had been there right under his nose the whole time. Never mind that Evan wasn't jealous; Hank still felt as though the entire episode disrespected the man he loved.

"Why not? You couldn't have bonded with her if you tried!" Evan smiled. "That was lust, man, old memories burbling up to unravel you. But you were already unraveling because of *me*, because of your proximity to the person your soul wanted to be with."

"Whatever you say," Hank said, shutting the back of the truck.

"You don't believe it?"

"Sure I do. I just don't know that we need to discuss it, or that you need to study it. Some things benefit from a little mystery, Captain."

Evan's smile made Hank want to kiss him, but instead Hank patted the side of the truck and said, "C'mon. Let's go."

Evan climbed into the passenger seat next to him and buckled his seat belt. "Nice sentiment, man. And I love you for it."

Hank sighed as he settled in for the next barrage of words from Evan. He could tell that Evan hadn't given up yet.

"But this isn't just about you, or me, or us. This is about coming to a better understanding of Alpha and Omega relationships, and how to best—"

Hank was grateful that his new cell phone rang. That is, until he picked it up. A woman's voice asked for Evan, without even introducing herself, as though she had a reason and a right to be calling Hank's personal number.

"Who's this?" he asked.

"Malena," she said, haughtily.

Handing the phone to Evan, he said, "Do you know someone named Malena?"

"Malena? Uh, yeah."

Hank could smell Evan's nervous-scent, nothing too overt, nothing that might cause an overreaction in Hank, but enough to raise his hackles. "Tell your ex-girlfriends not to call this number."

Evan rolled his eyes, like Hank was being ridiculous, but they'd been coming out of the woodwork since the show aired: women leaving messages on Evan's machine at school and at home, offering threesomes and more. It all had Hank very much on edge.

"Um, Mom?" Evan said, taking the phone.

Mom? Hank let out a breath. Of course! Evan's much-talked-about mother. Hank was surprised that he hadn't noticed the distinct lack of her actual presence in their lives during the last week, given how often Evan referred to her.

"You're here? In White Edge?" Evan's smile grew nearly manic with tension. "Well…oh, well…um, yeah, sure you can stay with us."

Hank's eyes nearly bugged out of his head. He and Evan were still fucking three or four times a day. He didn't see how the kid's mother could stay with them. That wasn't going to work out.

Evan caught his reaction and mouthed silently, "Just for a week, Hank! A week!"

At Hank's look of horror, Evan turned his attention back to the phone. "Yeah, um, Mom, well, you know things are still pretty intense between us. It could get a little crowded at our place. No! No, of course I'm not saying that you should stay in a hotel."

Hank tweaked his hearing so that he could hear Evan's mother's side of the conversation. Her voice was pleasant and reminded him of happy bells. "And to think, Evan, after all my protesting the pigs, you go and get bonded with one. How utterly unpredictable of you!"

"Yeah, Mom, I know." Evan laughed nervously. "So, just a week, right, Mom? And we'll need a lot of privacy."

"Oh, that'll be fine. I'm in the middle of a meditation practice that requires three hours a day of absolute dedication. Will that be enough time for you to have sex with your Alpha?"

Evan glanced up at Hank, obviously realized he was listening in, and broke into a nervous, silly grin. He pointed at the phone making crazy-person circles with his fingers. "Well, Mom, um, sure. I, uh, listen, let's not talk about that, okay? It's private. Between me and Hank."

"Oh, honey, everyone knows that you have to screw the Alpha all the time the first few months that you're bonded, right? I remember reading about that in college."

Hank groaned, and mouthed at Evan, "You have got to be kidding me."

"Uh, Mom, maybe you *should* get a hotel room," Evan said, his eyes half-closed in a strange kind of panic.

"But, Evan, we *never* see each other! It's been almost a year! A hotel is so impersonal! Just think, I get back from Bali to find that you've been on some reality program and have your very own Alpha to study—"

"Mom, I'm bonded to him. He's not my study."

"Well, how will you ever get your PhD, darling, if he's not your study?"

"Mom, uh, funny thing…but, hey. Let's talk about this later. Okay? I can't wait for you to meet Hank."

"So, I'll be staying at your place."

Hank shook his head madly, making cutting gestures at his throat.

Evan shot him some wild eyes and then said, "Sure, Mom, um, just, you know, privacy."

"Right, of course, dear. Privacy."

Hank blinked.

Evan hung up the phone saying, "It's just a week. And she's my mom. And we'll find a way around it. It's not like she'll be in our shower, right? Or our bed?"

Hank gripped the steering wheel tightly, and said, "Are you

sure? It sounds like you and your mom are pretty close."

"Ew, Hank. Disgusting."

"Just sayin', Evan."

"And I'm just sayin' that's a low blow, my brother."

"Sure you want to call me brother right now, Captain?"

Evan laughed, the sweet scent of his sweat filling Hank's lungs. Evan rubbed his hands along his thighs, the chafe of his palms against his blue jeans already a familiar sound to Hank. "So, what do we do now?"

Hank glanced into his rear-view mirror as he merged into traffic. "We go home, unpack these boxes, prepare for your mother's invasion, make love, and then, tomorrow, we go into the station. To fight crime."

"Do I get a cape?"

"No, the cape's for me."

Evan's eyes lit up with amusement. "I don't know. I think a cape might make you look a little gay, Hank."

"I think you make me look a little gay, sweetheart."

Evan grinned, his body easing comfortably into the seat. "Fighting crime. Sounds exciting, man."

Hank glanced over as Evan looked at him with such open adoration that Hank wanted to pull over and kiss his eyes, his lips, his cheeks, and every bit of his face. Instead he simply said, "It will be."

Evan looked around as though really understanding where he was and who he was with for the first time, and said, "Cool."

"Yeah, cool."

As they took the ramp onto the freeway, they passed a billboard advertising the next season of *OMEGA MINE: Search for a Soulmate.* Hank reached out and rested his hand lightly against the back of Evan's neck.

"Hmm?" Evan asked.

"Omega mine."

Evan glanced toward the sign and then leaned over to press a kiss to Hank's cheek. "Yeah, Hank. Omega yours. Forever."

THE END

Letter from Leta

Dear Reader,

Thank you so much for reading *Omega Mine: Search for a Soulmate*! I originally wrote this novel almost ten years ago and in 2018 decided to publish it under the pen name Halsey Harlow. I have since decided to retire that pen name and am re-releasing it as Leta Blake. I had so much fun writing this fluffy story of a bear shifter police officer finding his destined omega match. I hope you enjoyed reading it as much as I enjoyed crafting it.

Be sure to follow me on BookBub or Goodreads to be notified of new releases. And look for me on Facebook for snippets of the day-to-day writing life, or join my Facebook Group for announcements and special giveaways. To see some sources of my inspiration, you can follow my Pinterest boards or Instagram.

If you enjoyed the book, please take a moment to leave a review! Reviews not only help readers determine if a book is for them, but also help a book show up in site searches.

Also, for the audiobook connoisseurs out there many of my other books are also in audio. Most are narrated by fan favorites Michael Ferraiuolo or John Solo. I hope to eventually add my entire backlist to my audiobook roster over the next few years.

Thank you for being a reader!
Leta

Book 1 in the Home for the Holidays series

MR. FROSTY PANTS

by Leta Blake

Frosty former friends get a steamy second chance in this Christmas gay romance!

Can true love warm his frozen heart?

When Casey Stevens went away to college four years ago, he ghosted on his straight best friend, Joel Vreeland. He hoped time and distance would lessen the unrequited affection he felt, but all it did was make him miss Joel more.

Home for the holidays, Casey hopes they might find a way to be friends again. But Joel's frosty reception reminds Casey of just how hard he had to fight to be Joel's friend in the first place. It's going to take a Christmas miracle to get past that cool façade again.

Joel isn't as straight as Casey believes, and his years of pining for Casey have left him hurting and alone, caring for his abusive father and struggling to get by. Unable to trust anyone except his rescue dog—and with no reason to believe Casey is interested in him for more than a holiday fling—Joel's icy heart might shatter before it can thaw.

Can Casey and Joel's love overcome mistrust, parental rejection, class differences, and four long years apart? *Mr. Frosty Pants* is a stand-alone, Christmas gay romance by Leta Blake featuring a virgin hero, childhood friends-to-lovers, second chance romance, and steamy mm first times.

COWBOY SEEKS HUSBAND
by Leta Blake & Indra Vaughn

Walker Reed's Louisiana cattle ranch is in debt after costly repairs from hurricane damage. To get the money, his family schemes to make Walker the star of a new bachelor reality series: *Queer Seeks Spouse*. How hard can it be to fake interest in a dozen handsome men for a few weeks in exchange for enough money to solve all of their problems?

Roan Carmichael never got his Masters degree after his mother was diagnosed with cancer. With medical bills piling up, and a costly experimental treatment available, Roan signs on to be a suitor on *Queer Seeks Spouse*. While he hates having to leave his sick mother long enough to win the cash for her treatment, he's willing to do whatever it takes.

Can two men who are just in it for the money fake their way into real and lasting love?

Cowboy Seeks Husband, the latest book by *Vespertine* authors Leta Blake and Indra Vaughn, features a cowboy, a hipster, opposites attract, steamy scenes, and heart tugging moments that will leave you wanting more.

Standalone novel

SMOKY MOUNTAIN DREAMS
by Leta Blake

Sometimes holding on means letting go.

After giving up on his career as a country singer in Nashville, Christopher Ryder is happy enough performing at the Smoky Mountain Dreams theme park in Tennessee. But while his beloved Gran loves him exactly the way he is, Christopher feels painfully invisible to everyone else. Even when he's center stage he aches for someone to see the real him.

Bisexual Jesse Birch is a single dad with no room in his life for dating. Raising two kids and fighting with family after a tragic accident took his children's mother, he doesn't want more than an occasional hook-up. He sure as hell doesn't want to fall hard for his favorite local singer, but when Christopher walks into his jewelry studio, Jesse hears a new song in his heart.

Smoky Mountain Dreams is a heartfelt gay romance with a single dad, winter holiday highlights, found family, and steamy scenes to warm even the coldest heart!

TRAINING SEASON

by Leta Blake

Can a cowboy's firm hand help discipline this feisty figure skater—on and off the ice?

Matty Marcus fears he doesn't have what it takes to achieve his Olympic dream. His self-esteem is at an all-time low after figure skating coaches and skating judges have told him he's not skinny enough, good enough, or masculine enough to win.

Matty wishes he could afford the kind of coach he needs, a top-notch one who specializes in keeping their skaters focused. But those coaches are ridiculously expensive, and Matty is financially strapped.

Until a lucrative house-sitting gig brings him to rural Montana.

And to Rob.

No one has ever looked at Matty the way rural cowboy Rob Lovely looks at him. No one has ever touched him, loved him, and healed him from the inside out. No one has ever made him feel so valuable and adored. Worthy. Strong.

No one has ever taught Matty how to fly. Or how to lose.

Rob might be a cowboy and a single dad who knows nothing about figure skating, but after only a few months, he's trained a new kind of bravery into Matty's soul.

But to achieve his Olympic dream, Matty will have to face the ultimate test. Has he truly learned what it means to win—on and off the ice—during his training season?

Training Season is a MM romance with a feisty, flamboyant figure skater and an easy-going dominant cowboy, opposites attract, hurt-comfort, single dad, winter holiday highlights, love beyond reason, multiple steamy scenes, and a well-earned happy ending. *This book contains some BDSM elements.*

ANY GIVEN LIFETIME

He'll love him in any lifetime.

Neil isn't a ghost, but he feels like one. Reincarnated with all his memories from his prior life, he spent twenty years trapped in a child's body, wanting nothing more than to grow up and reclaim the love of his life.

As an adult, Neil finds there's more than lost time separating them. Joshua has built a beautiful life since Neil's death, and how exactly is Neil supposed to introduce himself? As Joshua's long-dead lover in a new body? Heartbroken and hopeless, Neil takes refuge in his work, developing microscopic robots called nanites that can produce medical miracles.

When Joshua meets a young scientist working on a medical project, his soul senses something his rational mind can't believe. Has Neil truly come back to him after twenty years? And if the impossible is real, can they be together at long last?

Any Given Lifetime is a stand-alone, slow burn, second chance gay romance by Leta Blake featuring reincarnation and true love. This story includes some angst, some steam, an age gap, and, of course, a happy ending.

Gay Romance Newsletter

Leta's newsletter will keep you up to date on her latest releases and news from the world of M/M romance. Join the mailing list today and you're automatically entered into future giveaways. letablake.com

Leta Blake on Patreon

Become part of Leta Blake's Patreon community in order to access exclusive content, deleted scenes, extras, bonus stories, rewards, prizes, interviews, and more. www.patreon.com/letablake

Other Books by Leta Blake

Any Given Lifetime
The River Leith
Smoky Mountain Dreams
Angel Undone
Omega Mine: Search for a Soulmate
Bring on Forever

The Home for the Holidays Series
Mr. Frosty Pants
Mr. Naughty List

The Training Season Series
Training Season
Training Complex

Heat of Love Series
Slow Heat
Alpha Heat
Slow Birth
Bitter Heat

'90s Coming of Age Series
Pictures of You
You Are Not Me

Stay Lucky Series
Stay Lucky
Stay Sexy

Co-Authored with Indra Vaughn
Vespertine
Cowboy Seeks Husband

Co-Authored with Alice Griffiths
The Wake Up Married serial
Will & Patrick's Endless Honeymoon

Gay Fairy Tales
Co-Authored with Keira Andrews
Flight
Levity
Rise

Leta Blake writing as Blake Moreno
The Difference Between
Heat for Sale

Audiobooks
Leta Blake at Audible

Free Read
Stalking Dreams

Discover more about the author online:
Leta Blake
letablake.com

About the Author

Author of the bestselling book Smoky Mountain Dreams and the fan favorite Training Season, Leta Blake's educational and professional background is in psychology and finance, respectively. However, her passion has always been for writing. She enjoys crafting romance stories and exploring the psyches of made up people. At home in the Southern U.S., Leta works hard at achieving balance between her day job, her writing, and her family.